,

About the authors

Sean O'Brien has published four award-winning collections of poems, most recently *Downriver*, which won the 2002 Forward Prize for Best Collection. His essays have been collected in *The Deregulated Muse: Essays on Contemporary British and Irish Poetry* (Bloodaxe) and he has translated Aristophanes' *The Birds* (Methuen). He was editor of *The Firebox: Poetry in Britain and Ireland After 1945*, and currently lives in Newcastle.

Jean Sprackland's first collection of poetry, *Tattoos for Mothers Day* (Spike), was shortlisted for the Forward Prize in 1999. Her second collection, *Hard Water* (Cape) was shortlisted for the Whitbread Award for Poetry and the T S Eliot Prize in 2004. She lives in Southport.

Tim Cooke has worked variously as a lecturer, an internet consultant, and a composer of music for film and television. His unpublished novel 'The Zero-Sum Game' was the source for the 2004 film *The Principles of Lust* directed by Penny Woolcock. This is his first major publication.

ellipsis
#1

Sean O'Brien

Jean Sprackland

Tim Cooke

First published in Great Britain in 2005 by Comma Press
www.commapress.co.uk
Distributed by Carcanet Press
www.carcanet.co.uk

'Rollercoaster Cowboy' first appeared in *Manchester Stories 5: Caesura* (Comma);
'Blue Guitar' and 'I Cannot Cross Over' in *Hyphen* (Comma), 'The Priest' in
Bracket (Comma), 'Tabs' in *Newcastle Stories 1* (Comma) and 'The Custodian' in
Phantoms at the Phil (Side Reel Press).

A CIP catalogue record of this book is available from the British Library.

ISBN 0-9548280-2-X

Lyrics from 'Loki' Daryl Hougen. Reprinted by permission.

The publisher gratefully acknowledges assistance from the Arts Council England
North West, and also the support of Literature Northwest, which is itself assisted
by ACE NW and CIDS (The Creative Industries Development Service).

Set in Baskerville 11/13 by XL Publishing Services, Tiverton
Printed and bound in England by SRP Ltd, Exeter

Contents

JEAN SPRACKLAND

The Other Man   1
Three Villages   5
Do You Read Swedish?   19
Rollercoaster Cowboy   29
Blue Guitar   37

TIM COOKE

The Priest   45
The Letter K   57
The Long Drive   73
Sweet Peas   85
Shopping List   91
Transparency   99

SEAN O'BRIEN

I Cannot Cross Over   113
Tabs   125
The Custodian   139
Three Fevers   151
Kiss Me Deadly on the Museum Island 161

JEAN SPRACKLAND

The Other Man

He cannot recall the name of this town. He steps out of the hotel bathroom, wrapped in a towelling robe. He stands at the window, in the exaggerated hush of the air-conditioning. He scans the windswept promenade and the empty beach below, hoping for clues.

He crosses the room to the bed, where his briefcase lies waiting. Cambridge Tan: not an ideal match with any of his suits, but the choice of his wife, a birthday gift. She loves to give him expensive things. It's made of the super-soft leather they call Italian Silk. When he strokes the case, he thinks of her skin, or at least he thinks of a woman's skin, a woman lying ready on a hotel bed. She doesn't quite honestly have a face, but he borrows his wife's face and pins it on firmly. He stands for a moment, enjoying the low shine of the leather under the lamp. Then he touches the brass catches with his thumbs and they spring open. The lid lifts with a sigh, like a dress pushed up over the thighs.

The click of the catches under his efficient thumbs is heard all over the hotel. In the room next-door a woman touches her best friend's husband's mouth to silence him. *What was that? Don't be so jumpy. You're making me nervous.* He licks her fingers and promises her something. Three floors down, a man in the shower – soaping his balls, rinsing off the sweat and boredom of the day, allowing the steam and the sting to augur well for the evening – leans round the curtain and calls *Hello, is someone there?* In the lobby, the receptionist tapping details on a keyboard feels the desk quake under her wrists, but only thinks it's time she went home, time she got a new job. A man at the bar sees the tremor in his glass: it's like that scene in Jurassic Park, he thinks, the first sign of something bad. Then he takes a long drink, and forgets.

Now the case lies spread on the bed, exposed, and a warm scent rises, a scent which reminds him he has a home. The interior is lined with green leather. There are hidden pockets the adept can find quickly with his fingers. These places are stitched and sequestered to meet the peculiar needs of the businessman on trips away from home. Like the bedside phone, the briefcase is discreet; it will hold your secrets for as long as you need it to. Tucked inside these soft folds, a few private comforts, depending on individual preference: phone numbers, contraceptives, something in liquid or powder form to keep out the cold and the dark. But never this: wrapped in a foreign cloth, like someone else's picnic.

There must have been a mix-up. Cases swapped, the classic thing. Now he thinks of it, the catches did feel fractionally harder – they resisted, sprang a little less eagerly. His case is new; how has it acquired this scuffmark? Perhaps the scent he breathed just now was of someone else's home, not his. Yes, someone has picked up his case by mistake. Another man who shares his taste for handcrafted leather, who has a wife as loving and generous as his own.

He hesitates, loath to touch, knowing already it will not be good. Then, braced for a shock, he handles the cloth parcel, lifts it out and unwraps it on the bed.

Bones.

He knows they are human. He has seen sheep bones and rabbit bones on country walks, has dug up cow bones in his garden, has torn meat from chicken and turkey bones. These are different. One he thinks is a rib, one a forearm (he wants to say *ulna* or *radius*). This sort of notched plate must come from the pelvis. Some long elegant fingers or toes, a few white oddments like pebbles. What slim pieces we break down into! He kneels by the bed and touches each one, arranges them

2

this way and that on the blue satin. They are dry, smooth, surprisingly clean. So clean they must have been boiled, he thinks with a shudder, imagining some terrible kitchen: bin bags, body parts, the whine of an electric carving knife, neighbours complaining about the smell. He sniffs the bones: they smell of nothing now, of absolute zero.

What kind of man attends a national conference with bones in his briefcase? A murderer? An accomplice at least: in concealment, disposal of the body, perverting the course of justice… he paces the room, picturing the conference suite, the delegates, trying to summon each face in turn to the witness-stand and cross-examine it.

This is no accident, he thinks. It's an icy realisation: some killer has palmed the evidence off on him. He has checked him out: knows his whereabouts, the make and colour of his case. Now this monster possesses his papers, the photo of his wife, his little comforts. He imagines his open case on another man's bed, and all his private things spread naked there. He sees the other man's fingers exploring its pockets and folds.

As the doors close behind him, he wonders briefly whether hotel lifts are fitted with security cameras. On further inspection he decides that the device in the ceiling is actually a smoke detector: lighting a cigarette is the only crime that matters here. All other offences go undetected. He feels like a time-traveller, snug in his capsule, gliding down a blind shaft between worlds. Thirty seconds of absolute freedom, in a space little bigger than a coffin but made to look infinite with mirrors. When he stares into that lit passage, and sees his own hollow face staring back, he remembers his purpose here. The doors part with a chime like an old-fashioned clock, marking his return to the world.

The corridor on the seventh floor stretches away empty. He opens the case, takes out the cloth parcel and places it carefully on the carpet outside room 701. Someone else will find it – someone who knows what to do. He takes the stairs, with the case – his but not his – swinging light and awkward

3

against his thigh.

Back in his room, he examines it closely. It will do. The scuffmark may come out with a bit of brown shoe-polish. He opens and shuts the lid, grieving a little over the stiffness of the catches. But he knows he will get used to them, and his wife will never notice. He will get a reprint of the little photo of her, and match up the silver pen and retractable pencil set. He will ask his secretary for copies of everything.

Three Villages

I

They found three last year: one drowning, two murders. One of them dated back twelve years: the husband panicked, he needed to get rid of her quick, so he drove her here from Leeds because it's easy digging. I imagine him throwing the shovel in the boot, thinking *It's over.* But this ground is not fixed and solid. Sand is unreliable stuff; it shifts and settles...

I hear coughing and there's Dr Quinn, leaning against a tree, smoking. He coughs all the time, like a kid teaching himself to smoke. The lifelong learning centre is no smoking of course – I'm surprised he can last a two-hour class. I wonder how old he is. He looks about fifty but that could be the fags – his skin's not at all good.

Morning Janet, he says in that rattly voice, stubbing out his cigarette carefully on the tree-trunk and putting it away in his pocket. He's considerate. And it's very nice of him to come out on a Sunday to show me the way. As soon as I showed an interest, he offered.

It's raining gently: we can hear it, but we stay dry under the trees. We walk, and I prattle on about murders and drownings and ask him whether he heard about the poor girl from Leeds.

Mobile dunes, he says, halting to light up again. There's nothing holding them down, nothing but marram grass. He asks did I know there was a law passed in the 1600s 'for the more effectual protection of the Starr'. That's what they called marram back then. The law forced tenants to plant a certain amount of it each year, and made it illegal to harvest any without permission. There were men called hawslookers whose job it was to catch people collecting the stuff.

By now we're out on the open dunes. What a lot of trouble to go to, I say, brushing the spiky blades with the palm of my hand.

Yes well, he says, it's the only thing keeping all this together. He waves his cigarette hand in the direction of the road and the housing estate. Remember the parable, Janet? The man who built his house on sand? Two thousand years on, we're still making the same mistake.

I'm so glad we arranged to meet here. I don't think I could bear Dr Quinn to see where I live. It's at the classier end, in a cul-de-sac, but nevertheless. They throw them up cheap, of course. You only have to walk down the roads and look at them – ten years on and they're standing at some crazy angles. And the roads are all full of bumps and dips. I imagine he lives in one of those big double-fronted Victorian places in town, untidy but full of character. It'll be lined with books and he'll have high ceilings and a proper fireplace. He won't know what it's like here: how everything gets sandblasted, how you have to paint your woodwork every two years, how if you park a new car outdoors it starts to rust within six months. You sweep sand out of the porch, off the windowsills – in summer it gets right into the house, you even find it in the kitchen cupboards. You see it swirling away down the plughole when you wash your hair; your eyes and mouth are gritty with it.

How much further, Dr Quinn? I sound like a child: *are we nearly there yet?* I want to add that as far as I'm concerned we can walk all day, it's fine by me.

Not far now, he coughs. You do understand, don't you, it'll be approximate? Even we academics are by no means certain. I'm afraid we just don't have definitive documentary evidence. He tries to avoid a big lump of dog dirt, and fails.

He's wearing completely unsuitable shoes – sort of brogues. You'd think someone like him would have a pair of walking boots. We're going on hand-drawn maps, he says, we know they're incomplete. There's room for some serious research, it just needs someone to take it on.

He leads the way onto a very steep path up the side of a high dune. This is hard on the legs, he's very slow ahead of me and it really gets him coughing, but we make it to the top. There's a good view across the sea towards North Wales. The rain's stopped, the sky's cleared, I can see the Clwyddian Range and the pale but unmistakable shape of Snowdon behind.

He slumps onto the sand, and I sit down too, get out my water bottle. When he's got his breath back, he says Well, Janet, have you thought any more about the university?

There's a bit of a silence while I think how to reply. He's leaning on one elbow and looking at me very intently. He has unusual eyes, the colour of malt whisky, and flecks of peat in them.

I don't know, I say, it's a difficult time... I think my, um, I don't think Frank's too keen. I seem to have developed an allergy to the word *husband*.

It's true: Frank doesn't want me to go to university. He thinks it's silly, a waste of time (it's funny really, because he was always dead keen for Tim to go). He was fine with this when it was just a hobby – evening class once a week, a bit of reading in between. Now he can see I'm serious, and he doesn't like it. He's started to call me Professor. Come on then Prof, he says, tell us the meaning of life. It's 42, don't you know that? Even I know that, and I haven't got two O'Levels to rub together. He thinks it's hilarious. I'm surprised he can go on being so jovial, under the circumstances.

Dr Quinn sighs and says Change can be threatening for some people, but there's no escaping it. Change is what History is all about.

I consider going home and repeating this to Frank, but decide against it.

Change. There's a lot of it about at the moment. I always thought my job was to keep things steady. Stability: that was my guiding principle, no matter what. I've spent twenty years forcing doors and windows shut, holding lids down, barring all the exits. I'm not the only one who's paid the price. Now Tim's gone, lost, and I've only got me. I asked him *Was it a cry for help?* but he just walked out and slammed the door.

Dr Quinn is lying flat out and has lit another cigarette. He's the only person I know who still smokes the mentholated kind these days. He takes long desperate drags, as though it's pure nourishment.

Have you always been interested in the past, Dr Quinn? I feel a bit shy asking – it's the first time I've ever asked him anything. Also it's not really one of the questions I want to ask, which are things like *Do you live alone, How old are you and Can I call you Steve?* It makes me shy because I think he can probably hear all those questions rolled up inside the one I've just asked.

He goes on smoking and staring at the sky.

Then he starts telling me about a school trip to some castle or other when he was ten years old. They were allowed to go off and explore. Everyone else made for the tower, racing to the top, pushing and shoving on the spiral staircase.

I stayed on the ground, he says. I don't, I'm not, heights are not my thing. I walked all the way round the foot of the tower, looking at the stonework, seeing how it was made. There was lots of graffiti – some scratched in with a penknife – you know, *Baz woz ere* – and some much older, carved with real skill. I found a set of initials – RWN – and the date 1580. It was made four hundred years ago and it was just *there* in front of me, I could put my fingers in and feel the marks. It made me dizzy. The others came charging down the staircase and straight into the gift shop. Except for one boy, who'd been sick at the top…

He grins suddenly. I can't help noticing he has really bad teeth.

You didn't tell them? I ask. You didn't show anyone else?

He sits up and grinds the cigarette stub into the sand. He rubs his face all over with his hand.

No, he says.

We're sitting so close, I can smell him. Smoke and rain, the damp wool of his old donkey-jacket, and something else, something irresistibly sad. I breathe it in, hold it. The moment spreads, time is stretchy, almost liquid. I stare at his hand, his stained fingers.

Let's get moving, he says, it's clouding up again.

So this is the place. He's thirty yards away, pacing a circle in the sand. A village was lost here. Records show that sometime between 1543 and 1588 (the sources don't agree; Dr Quinn says this is quite commonplace), there was a giant sandblow here, and a whole village was buried, never to be found again. No one has ever seen so much as a chimney. But it's here, right under our feet.

All it would take is some serious digging, I shout, with proper machinery!

I don't think he heard me. He's pacing the shape and size of it, sketching an outline in the sand, pausing here and there and scuffing a series of depressions with his foot. It looks far too small for a village. It's like standing on a building site and looking at the foundations for a new house: the rooms are so tiny, you can't believe people will live in them. He takes out a handful of little plastic sticks and pushes them into the depressions. Then he moves from one marker to the next, pointing his electronic measuring gadget: point and *beep*, point and *beep*. Now he shuffles along the same route, head bowed, eyes fixed on the ground, examining every inch of the terrain like a detective making a fingertip search of a crime scene.

I'm imagining what it must have been like. They were

adaptable people whose world was not fixed or solid. They understood the shifting landscape around them; their cottages creaked and subsided on the unreliable ground. They knew all about sandstorms too… but this one was different, a blizzard like nothing they'd seen before. The wind had been howling and rattling for days, there was no let-up. Sand was drifting in doorways; they had to climb out of windows, with children in their arms and whatever belongings they could carry. They wrapped their faces in rags to keep it out of their eyes and mouths. The sky was dark with it, the air was choking. It was devouring their village and nothing could stop it. They looked back one last time and –

You ought to take that degree, he says in a low wheeze. He's very close. He touches my sleeve with his fingertips and looks straight at me with those unreadable eyes. You have *quality of mind*, he says. He takes a fierce drag on his cigarette and turns away, convulsing with something almost but not quite a cough.

Then he's back to his pacing, and I'm so happy I kneel and scoop up handfuls of lovely sand. I squeeze it hard in my fists and watch it spill: millions of hard shiny uncompromising grains, rubbing and squeaking against one another, no give in them, and each one light as dust.

II

You know what you need? says Dave. Peripherals.

Peripherals? I haven't got a clue, and it's no good pretending with Dave. We were at school together, he can read me like a book.

You know, he says, some machines. Arcade games. Kiddie rides. And an ice-cream kiosk.

It's a model village, I say, not Blackpool Tower.

He takes a swig of his tea and grimaces. Bloody hell Frank, he says, I know times are hard – you recycling the teabags now?

The sun comes out and we sit in silence for a minute, enjoying the warmth. I can feel my spirits lift. It's only February, but a day like this gives you faith.

The punters, he says, granted they come to see the little houses, the little train, the itsy-bitsy village green with its little morris dancers – I don't like his sarky tone, I raise a hand but he continues – but they're on holiday, Frank. They come with their pockets full of lovely holiday money, all ready to spend it on candy-floss and treats. You're missing an opportunity to oblige them. So they go down the pier and blow it there instead.

Dave, Dave, you're missing the point, I insist, this is a classy place, a family attraction. Somewhere for the grandparents to bring the kids. I flap my hand towards the village, but of course it's all covered up for the winter, hibernating under its blue tarpaulins.

I know, mate, nods Dave, but what's your alternative? All this Merrie England doesn't pay its way. He picks up his mug, turns it thoughtfully to and fro. Mugs, he says. Tea-towels, keyrings, car stickers. A little shop selling all the tat…

I sigh. Have you any idea what that would cost me? Extra staff, fixtures and fittings.

I wish he'd give it a rest. I actually wish he'd piss off. I just want to be left alone for twenty minutes to sit in the sun and think about nothing.

The sunshine makes me remember the good times. How Tim used to like this place. When he was just a boy, I mean, long before it all kicked off. He used to come with me at weekends. You'd think it would be the miniature railway he'd have gone for – all lads like trains don't they? But no, what he really loved was the row of shops. It's a proper old-fashioned village and there's one of every kind: baker, grocer, butcher, hairdresser, milliner, haberdasher (we had a daft little game with the word *haberdasher*, it made him laugh every time). There's a sign at the farm down the road saying NEW LAID EGGS. Everything within walking distance. If you look closely, you'll see that every single villager is smiling: even the steeplejack, even the burglar being handcuffed by the local bobby.

He wanted to help with the repainting, but I drew the line at that – it's a delicate job, easy to make mistakes. The Dog & Gun, for instance. It's not just the doors and window-frames; there's a tiny pub sign too: a hunting dog sleeping by a log fire, with a rifle under his paws. You use a special brush the size of a cocktail stick. You need a steady hand.

It's one of my favourite pieces. The windows are made of yellow plastic, so it looks cosy and lit from within. If you kneel down and squint a bit, you can really imagine it's your own friendly local. No loud music, no binge drinking. Just the crackle of a log fire, the clatter of dominoes, a couple of old blokes at the bar with their proper pints and the smell of pipesmoke. Jesus, I'd fall through that door and you wouldn't be seeing me again.

You OK, Frank? Dave has put on a comical pair of sunglasses. They're like antiques. The lenses are covered in scratches – I'm surprised he can see through them at all.

I consider spilling the beans: telling him Tim's gone, for good this time, and Janet's taking it hard. But I just can't bring myself to say it. Dave's life isn't easy: he used to have his own hotel, and now he works behind the bar in someone else's, and his wife left him in 1996 and took his daughter to live in Spain.

Just thinking about what you said, I lie, the gift shop and all that.

Yeah well, think it over, he says happily. You don't want to end up like me, slogging my guts out for the benefit of some other fat bastard.

He knows I've had an offer. Laughable he called it. It's the fairground: they want to pay me off, get me out of the way so they can drive straight through this place with a JCB. Send them packing, Dave told me. Them and their fancy new rollercoaster. Tell 'em to stick it.

When I took this place on, Dave was one of the few people who didn't fall about laughing. Janet's brother knew some cousin of the bloke who was selling up. The place had been derelict when he bought it, and it was derelict five years later. He'd had dreams of refurbishing and re-opening, but before he could get started he developed cancer of the colon and that was the end of that.

I took it on as a business proposition. I went to the bank and negotiated a loan, got Janet to write up a business plan and budgets and everything. I loved the idea of being my own boss. And I thought it would be something to pass on to Tim. A family business.

Maybe they were right to laugh. You wear yourself out making everything right for your son. He grows up clever, good-looking. One or two nice girlfriends. Then bang! For no apparent reason, he loses it. Shuts himself in his room. Says nothing. Stares out the window all day.

Janet took him to the doctor and he said depression. He's seventeen, I said. What could he possibly have to be depressed about? The doctor gave him pills but we don't think he took them. He was supposed to have counselling but he wouldn't go –

I'll be off then, says Dave, pocketing the awful sunglasses. The sun's gone in. He nods in the direction of the blue tarpaulins. What's new this season, Frank?

I've added at least one new feature every year. Last year it was the children's swing park. There's a roundabout and a slide and a sandpit. An old-fashioned pram is parked beside the bench, and a smiley mother is sitting with her baby on her knee, watching the children play.

This year, I haven't got round to it. What with everything else. Janet and I used to work on the ideas together. But all she wants to talk about these days is us, our marriage. Then she goes out and walks on the sand dunes all day… at least that's where she says she's been. I nipped out to the porch and checked her boots once or twice, and they did have sand on them.

Now she's keen on history all of a sudden. She's been doing a course, reading some deadly boring books. The other night I was getting into bed and she said Frank, I want to go to university. I laughed and said You're forty years old, love! She switched off the light then and wouldn't say anything else.

I should be more tactful, I know. She's had a hard time. She's the one who came home and found him. She used to say she could see it when she closed her eyes: the trail of blood across the kitchen floor and onto the patio…

I told her Let it go, you can't change the past.

Anyway, I said, you heard what the paramedic said. He was never in any danger – he cut them the wrong way.

III

The wind's vicious, and the boy has no gloves – his hands are icy even inside his coat pockets. Nevertheless there's an ice-cream van parked on the sand. It must be the weekend. Surface water races glinting over the sand towards him, and he feels as though he's inside a computer game.

He aches with cold; he longs to get back indoors. He lives at the arse-end of nowhere, yet that's his happiest moment, when he gets inside and locks the door. The wind comes straight off the sea, hyperactive on rain, sleet and hail. The place rattles all day and all night. It's like being on a ship.

He sits for hours in the window, wrapped in a sleeping bag, scanning the place with the binoculars. He studies the perimeter fence made of concrete panels, the three rows of barbed wire with bits of shredded plastic caught in it; the blackened place where they have fires and try to burn stuff that doesn't burn properly; the cage full of wheelie-bins. There's a few old fridges left out to rust, even though you're meant to dispose of them carefully because of the CFCs. A stainless steel sink unit, a heap of pallets, a shattered phone box lying on its side with the payphone still inside.

The chalets have wooden balconies and satellite dishes, flat roofs that let the rain in. When he was a kid, he and his mates used to sneak in in the winter, climb up the fire-escapes and run about on the roofs. It was pure fun. There were gaps to jump over, and scary bits that sagged when you stepped on them. Now they have lights and security guards, you'd never get away with it. There's even a lookout tower, like on the Berlin Wall. It's an abseil tower really, but if anyone comes looking for him he'll climb up and shoot at them. Unless it's Shona...

But he knows Shona won't come. She's got a new boyfriend, she told him last time he rang. She said *Don't call again, or I'll put him on.*

15

His friend Rob suggested this place. Winter let, dirt cheap. His sister lived there with her boyfriend a couple of winters ago, while they were house-hunting. On his furtive walks after dark, the boy has found the entertainment complex, boarded up for the winter, with signs to the Cash Bonanza Bingo, the Crazy Croc children's soft play area, and the Cock & Bull Family Fun Pub. There's no one else around except Maintenance, who lives in a caravan behind the boiler-house and always wears the same red check lumberjack shirt.

Most days the boy just stays indoors, keeps his head down. When he needs stuff, he goes to Kwik Save and brings back as much as he can carry. Cheap food is very heavy: tinned stuff, potatoes, frozen meat. He knows he shouldn't really buy frozen because he's only got a little icebox, but if you keep it in the fridge and eat it quick it's fine.

When the sky clears he fixes the binoculars on the gas rig. It's an alien structure, a space station. He'd like to see the roustabouts working or staggering about the rig drunk, but the lenses aren't strong enough. Some days it's all misty and distant; other times, like today, so sharp and close he could swim out to it easily. At night it's warm and foreign with lights and he wants to step onto the sea and walk it.

The tideline stretches ahead of him like a road. The red flag's been flying ever since he got here, the wind's torn it to bits. It makes him think of a ragged filthy old flag he saw in a church once, years ago. The Sunday School teacher said it had been brought back from the battlefield. He felt sick thinking of all the blood and putrefying limbs and blown-up bodies and wondering what it meant, why they'd brought it into a church and hung it on the wall where people could see it while they were singing hymns and everything. He tried to ask his mum but she said Oh Timmy, don't talk about it, it's horrible.

Mum. He said he'd ring when he got settled, that must have been weeks ago. But she always wants to know why, and the harder she tries not to the more upset she gets. She wants it to be like when he was little: he'd tell her where it hurt, and she'd make it better.

When he was in hospital, Shona rang, and his mum answered and blurted it all out. Shona said she'd come and visit, but he knew she wouldn't. They didn't have that kind of relationship, in sickness and in health and all that. She was really pretty, Shona, but her front teeth were a bit crooked and she used to cover her mouth with her hand when she was talking. She'd lie stretched out on her mum's bed, laughing, trying to hide her teeth, and he'd have to get his clothes on and leave fast, or he'd jump back in with her and never leave at all.

Rob says she used the word *psycho*.

He's reached a place where the ground is completely made of razorshells. You can't take a step without breaking them. He stands there a long time, knees shaking.

They won't find him here, will they? He told them he'd get a B&B. There are hundreds of dives and dosshouses in this town.

The clouds part, and the sun throws down a precise single beam, like a helicopter searchlight.

Do You Read Swedish?

According to the internal report demanded by Head Office, Robert Maguire was discovered on Wednesday November 27th at 08.17, forty-three minutes before opening time. A junior member of staff, Miss Valeria Stubbs, encountered him as she arrived for work. She challenged him, and when he offered no explanation for his presence, she raised the alarm by pushing the panic button behind the Enquiries Desk.

It emerged that Mr Maguire had been there for almost three weeks. He had not been spotted by any one of the seventeen regular security guards on their overlapping shifts, neither had the state-of-the-art intruder system, with its trip-beams and cameras, detected his presence. No satisfactory explanation was given for this failure of procedures.

Valeria was having coffee with her brother. He had something to put to her.

'I've been thinking,' he said, gazing into his cup, 'about your future.'

'Do we have to talk about it?'

'You're throwing your life away.'

''You're being melodramatic.'

'Mum's worried. She always thought you'd go far.'

'Mum is not worried. She hasn't even looked at me properly for the past five years. Not since –'

'You need to get out of that house. Out of this place. You're a misfit.'

'Thanks –'

'You know what I mean. You're the clever one in the family. A'Levels and everything. You should be at university, studying to be a doctor.'

'Nick, my A'Levels are in English, French and Spanish. I don't think they'd have me on A & E.'

'Whatever. What I wanted to say is, if it's the money I can get it. Borrow it. You mustn't be held back.'

It was nice of him. Very nice. She should thank him. In fact for a split second she saw herself in a stripy college scarf, books under her arm, crossing a frosty quad. It looked all right….

She sighed. Where the hell did she get the word *quad*? Students get pissed, sleep around, run up debts. Only the other week she'd heard someone on the radio, some vicar or bishop or something, going on about students and how immoral they are, how promiscuous… he'd used the phrase *recreational sex*. Valeria had found this faintly disturbing.

'The thing is, I like my job.'

He laughed through his teeth. 'What's to like?'

She considered this, but all the things she thought of seemed impossible to communicate to Nick. He sat scowling, affronted by the noise, the muzak, the long queue of customers squabbling over trays. They were demolishing huge meals, leafing through catalogues and smacking their kids. He thought this was all there was. He would never understand about the delicious smell of the showroom, most noticeable after closing time when all the customers were gone and the air-conditioning had powered down. Then the store went back into its secret life, its dreamtime. The air was still and full of the scent of new wood and cloth. There was a different, softer acoustic. Valeria and the others padded about as if they were in their slippers. You could talk as you worked, though she preferred to find a task in a quiet corner near a window, looking straight out onto the traffic and weather of the M62. She loved it in winter: the black road rowdy and smeared with headlights, and the store locked tight, guarded, engrossed in its dream life.

'What would I want to go to university for? It would be a waste of money. I'm happy. I'm really fine. You don't have to be a doctor or a lawyer to be fine.' They sat in silence for a whole minute, maybe two. 'Nick, do you ever dream about her?'

He said nothing. He was fiddling with his mobile, pretending to check for messages.

'I do,' said Valeria. 'She's never in the dreams, but they are about her.'

He took off his glasses and rubbed his face all over with the palm of his hand. He looked odd without his glasses – wonky and a bit old.

'It was a long time ago, Vee. You can't let it ruin your whole life.'

The trees here are like machines in a shut-up factory. The leaves are scraps of steel, shorn off by the wind, clattering to the ground. The river is a strip of concrete, cars sucked along on the current. I'm trying to paddle a canoe through a contraflow, but the paddles are made of paper, all bendy and useless…

There were only three staff on the floor after closing. Joanna and Cy were over by the Order Point, flirting and laughing. They were all right, these two, but they had a way of making you feel surplus to requirements. Valeria started the rounds of the room-sets with the spray polish. She was rubbing at fingerprints on a glass-topped coffee table when she heard a scuffling sound from behind the partition. She stepped round and saw him. He was sitting on the floor behind a brown leather sofa, leaning out on one elbow and scanning the shopfloor. When he saw Valeria, he froze.

For a moment they simply looked at each other. Valeria wondered what the correct procedure might be. Should she go and find someone? That would mean leaving him, and you could be sure he wouldn't be here when she got back. She should probably shout for Cy. But it seemed crass somehow. Shouting would cut right through the lovely quiet. And perhaps this guy was insane, or on the run from the police. It would be important to stay calm. She said this to herself, but it was unnecessary; she was entirely calm.

'What do you want?' She was whispering, which she supposed was a bit odd.

'Nothing. Nothing. Leave me alone.' His own voice was low and furious. He darted back behind the sofa, and Valeria was left standing in the stillness, clutching the polish and duster. She stared at the antique stain dresser, the framed print of wet pebbles. At the corner of her eye, the window: lorries thundering through the spray. She took a breath, ready to speak, then let it out again. She turned and walked away towards Kitchens, where she found mess to clean up: someone had stuffed wet tissues into the pull-out larder fittings and spat chewing-gum into the sink.

Valeria's parents didn't talk anymore. They still met, once a day, at a table as heavy and mute as a church door. He propped his elbows, she spread her hands and looked at her fingernails. The table was a map of extreme terrain. Sometimes she traced contours and riverlines and scabs of wax like bombed cities.

Valeria lay awake, thinking about the man behind the sofa and wondering what he was doing now. Security would probably have caught him. She should have reported it right away. Whenever a member of staff reported a shoplifter, they got an extra half day off. But he's not a shoplifter, thought Valeria, I could tell that right away. And I don't want a half day off. I want to work weekends, nights, Bank Holidays, I don't ever want to stop.

The last time she heard them talk was Christmas Eve – not last year but the one before. She was making her way to bed early, like a child. Nick was out with friends, and she didn't want to sit in silence with the two of them. Her mother had fetched down the old Christmas tree from the attic and was hanging it with balding tinsel and dented baubles and all the other tat they'd had since way back when. Watching her, Valeria felt a tightness in her throat – a warning sign – but she didn't move fast enough. Her mother reached right to the bottom of the box and dug out two ancient homemade decorations – matching angels made from an old cereal packet. One with clumsy edges and wax crayon scribbled right over the lines, the other with careful features and a touch of glitter on the wings. She gave a weird cry and crumpled to her knees, grabbing the tree for support so that it rocked and jangled. Valeria slipped from the room. *I didn't see a thing.* Hurrying upstairs, she heard their voices: his low, hers broken. Once, this would have been the right thing: sharing the grief, talking it out. But it was too late now. They had chosen silence.

I cut a slot in the wet sand, step hard and feel the steel of the spade through the sole of my boot. I've dug so many holes, I'm bound to find her in the end. A sudden clink of glass – old-fashioned green glass. A bottle with a narrow waist and a loose metal clasp. I cut again to pare it from the sand and stones, but it shatters on the blade…

There had been a change of layout. This week the space was divided by a long, tall bookcase, and he was hiding behind it. He was looking at her through a gap. She was going to walk past, pretend she hadn't seen him, but it was too silly.

'What do you want?'

'I told you, nothing.'

'Well, what are you doing here? The store's closed.'

'Duh. I know that.' She stepped round the end of the bookcase and confronted him. He flinched, recovered. His face was in shadow. 'I love these books,' he said. He took one down from a shelf. An unpronounceable title, black lettering on white.

'Do you read Swedish?' said Valeria.

He shoved it back on the shelf. 'I like the look of them. They look clever. I skim through them.'

'You're living here, aren't you?'

'*Living*?' He spoke the word as if it was new to him.

'You'll be in real trouble if anyone sees you.'

He smiled then. She was on his side. She would not give him away. They were in it together.

His name was Robert, and he was sleeping in the furniture showroom: sometimes on the brown leather sofa, sometimes on one of the beds. There was one bed in particular – king-size, with a high wooden headboard and a red quilt. He felt very safe there, though he couldn't say why. There was just something about it. No, he wasn't *homeless*, he had a perfectly good house. In the daytime, he wandered round the store looking at things. Sometimes he sat in the restaurant, but the staff had started to greet him as if they knew him, and that was a worry, so he went outside and walked round the car-park, mooched about in Toys R Us or the tile superstore.

She asked him why he was sleeping in a fake living-room in a shop, when he had a living-room of his own.

'You know that road behind the tile place,' he said, 'the one that leads to that dismal yard? Hangar doors, a row of trucks backed up. I watch them loading these giant crates onto trolleys and wheeling them in. It goes on all day, the *beep-beep-beep* of the trucks reversing. I watch them, and I think what is all that stuff, who's buying it?' He shook his head. 'All day. *Beep-beep-beep.*'

Valeria heard Cy whistling. He sounded very close.

'Look,' she hissed, 'if you want me to keep quiet, the least you can do is tell me why you're here.'

He hesitated. His eyes were bloodshot. He rubbed his chin on his collar with a rasp of stubble. 'I don't know,' he said. 'There were fourteen break-ins on our street last year. The doctor gave me pills but I flushed them down the toilet. And

24

I like it here. Lovely furniture. You say fake, but all the stuff's real and much better than I could afford. Very clean.' She started to laugh and he rounded on her. 'It's different if you've got a family to go home to. I bet you've got a family?'

Valeria hesitated.

'Brothers? Sisters?'

'A brother. No sister.'

As Nick says, it was a long time ago.

A house. A hallway full of sand. An ice-cream van has got stuck near the front door, and a tractor comes to pull it out. The whole house stinks of seaweed and rubbish – broken plastic, bits of cheap toys that will never rot away. This house used to be the biggest place in the world... but today it's dark, squashed narrow as a letterbox that snaps shut when the rain starts...

Joanna was worried about Valeria. She'd been quiet recently and sometimes after closing time they couldn't find her.

'I'm not being funny, we all go AWOL from time to time, but if something's bothering you...'

'No. No, it's nothing, honest. I'm sorry. I've just been a bit tired. Not sleeping well. Sorry.'

'God, Valeria, you don't have to apologise to me. I'm not your boss. Just watch your back when Cy's around, that's all. He's asked where you are a couple of times. Don't worry, I covered for you.'

'Thanks. Thankyou. I'll do the same for you sometime.'

Joanna smiled. Where Cy was concerned she would never need to call in any favours from Valeria.

Valeria and Robert had been playing a sort of game: the store would close and she would go looking for him. He was usually inside one of the wardrobes, but he left no clue. She kept one eye on Kitchens, where Joanna was perched on the marble countertop with her legs dangling and Cy was leaning close, menacing her with a lime-green washing-up brush and making her squeal with laughter. Valeria went from one room to another, opening doors, braced again and again for the shock of him. It took her back to games of hide-and-seek with Nick and Kirsty, her heart thumping playfully, the blood scuttling through her veins. Her favourite hiding-place used to be the airing-cupboard: all order and warmth, water in the pipes making the odd quiet remark.

When at last she found him, they would talk in whispers. There was no time for preliminaries.

'Have you always lived alone?'

'There used to be someone. Have you never lived alone?'

'No, but I'd like to. Are you planning to stay here forever?'

'It's temporary. What did you think the first time you saw me? Were you scared?'

'Were you?'

'You look so tired all the time. Don't you sleep?'

'I dream a lot. Do you think our dreams tell us things?'

'What happened to your sister?'

She pulled back abruptly. After a moment she closed the wardrobe door quietly and walked away.

They stood at the window like a couple and looked out at the traffic.

'It's eight thirty,' said Valeria. 'You'd think rush hour would be over.'

'It's always rush hour,' said Robert. 'All day and all night. Why are you crying?'

She hid in the staff toilets until everyone else had gone. Then she and Robert lay on the king-sized bed. The room was cast in a low bluish light, it felt like a film set. At first she was anxious about the recreational sex, but they didn't touch. Then she told him all about Kirsty: the family holiday by the sea, the two of them down at the harbour fishing for crabs, her dad shouting when Valeria came back alone, the waiting, the police, the silence that had filled the house to the brim ever since. She told him about a fight just the day before, when she had pulled out a fistful of her sister's hair. She told him about the dreams, the trail of clues they seemed to leave. He said nothing at all, just held her in his arms. His clothes smelt hopeless but comforting.

The hum of a car engine, a rattly old Cavalier on a sunlit strip of road. Window cranked down to hear the first seagull, catch the taste of salt. And thank god – here's the house at last, right on the beach. How could I have forgotten it?

I've been away too long. The tide's right up, swirling over the step and under the door. It's so cold and damp inside, I'm trying to warm my hands at the fire… but there is no fire, just moss growing in the grate.

Now I can hear him walking on the roof. I knew I should never have told him about this place. He's stepping on the broken slates, which are thin and loose as shale. And she's here, sleeping in the other room. I've betrayed her once already. He mustn't wake her. I have to stop him breaking through…

The security lighting was still on when she woke. She slid out and tiptoed to the window. The traffic was at a standstill. There were messages on her phone. They would be worrying.

She looked back at the hunched shape on the bed, and beyond it the empty beds, their pillows and blankets never disarranged. Wardrobes and chests of drawers with nothing inside, neat bedside rugs, lamps, mirrors…

The evidence.

The lies.

He was part of it. Maybe she'd even invented him. Could you sleep with a figment of your imagination? Yes, she felt sure people did it all the time. He was no more real than the fresh-faced student with books under her arm.

He started to stir under the red quilt. She walked quickly, made it to Enquiries, reached a trembling hand under the desk and found the panic button.

Rollercoaster Cowboy

Designed by Charles Paige of the Pennsylvania Roller Coaster Company, and built from Nicaraguan pitch pine. Two trains, each consisting of four cars (including one backwards-facing) and able to carry 24 passengers per train.

Come on Coral, let's set our little row of fires.

Here, I'll screw the newspaper up nice and tight, stuff it in between the iron frame and the struts, and into the gaps between the planks here on the station (this part's all timber, it'll go like a bomb). I've brought a bit of petrol in a plastic bottle, I'll slosh it here and there. It hasn't rained for a good two weeks, everything's bone-dry, once it takes hold it'll spread like wildfire… Christ, I think I said that out loud, must be careful.

No problem with the matches, Coral – the air's so close. So still, I think I can hear the leopards pacing just the other side of the perimeter fence. Listen: one two three four five six seven turn, one two three four five six seven turn… do you think they know I'm doing this for them? For you too of course, Coral. And for myself… after all, how can I ever get anywhere, with this heap of rotting wood and scrap metal dragging on me?

You're not really here, of course, I know that. Think I'm stupid? There's a thread of smoke, very straight, a dead giveaway. Time to get out of here.

The arcade. Not Funland – too brash and brightly-lit, families bunched round the Penny Falls. One of these gloomy little dives on Nevill Street is more my style. As usual it's full of gormless youths, makes me feel ancient. Straight through to the back, never mind the flashing and the racket, make for the row of old one-arm bandits, the only thing in here worth the candle.

And the toilets – I'm bursting for a piss. Weak bladder – can't hold it like I used to. In my old record-breaking days I'd hang on all afternoon, then give Bill a signal to stop her while I ran for the bogs, or more often the bushes. People don't think about stuff like that. Like eating and drinking up on the ride. Once I timed it wrong with the flask of coffee, thought I glimpsed clots of it snatched and hanging in the air as we hit that second bend.

You know what, it's knackered me. Jesus, now I'm talking to the stinking urinal! *The doctor says my spine's shot, my brain's bruised like a peach. I can feel every little jolt I ever took. Hurts just to walk.*

Never used to notice it. I remember my first time: Margate, 1964, fifteen years old. As we creaked up the gradient I thought: This is it. The long moment suspended. Then full bat, and your guts chasing to catch up. I liked hearing the girls scream. I thought: There's a living to be made here. Most people go on a coaster a couple of times a year, max. It comes after the walk along the prom and before the ice-cream. But I was already thinking Guinness Book of Records. I was thinking chat shows, kids with autograph books, an advertising campaign or two. I saw myself travelling, riding them in Paris, America, Japan.

Shit, I've just caught sight of myself in that broken bit of mirror – a right pig's breakfast. Lighting a fag, flicking ash into the washbasin. What a joke. I've never even been abroad. And my nearest brush with fame and fortune was the British Vintage Endurance Record in '71: twelve days and nights. Every time we docked, Bill would sneak me a smoke and talk about the coaster: the history, the science, the craftsmanship. But after a week the screaming went flat, like canned laughter. All the girls started to look the same, queuing in short skirts and blotchy legs, in that icy wind that knifes its way through from the sea. Chewing, sticking bits of gum to the barrier, shouting out smutty remarks. One of them took off her knickers and threw them onto the track. Bill hooked them off with a jemmy and flicked them into the bushes. They fluttered there like a little pink flag 'til they got ripped to shreds in the gales a week later.

Eighteen metres high, eight hundred and twenty-five metres long, a great veteran of the golden age of wooden rollercoasters: not too wild and not too slow.

Coral. She's by the burger stand on the prom, staring up at the Cyclone and eating chips out of a polystyrene tray. She isn't wearing a short skirt, though it's a warmish day. She has on dirty jeans and men's boots and one of those big weatherproof coats explorers wear trekking across bloody Antarctica. There's about half a dozen stickers on it, all the same: CLOSE THE ZOO, and a smudgy picture of a grinning chimpanzee. Her red hair's blowing all over her face.

Christ knows what makes me stop and speak to her. Just the way she's looking up at it like that. She looks like someone who needs information, and no one knows the Cyclone like I do.

'Built in 1939,' I say, keeping it casual.

Her fierce green eyes focus on me a moment. 'Looks like it,' she says. 'Held together with rust.'

'Frame needs a lick of paint,' I have to admit. 'But it's mostly wooden.'

'I can see that,' she says.

I say nothing for a minute, feeling a bit daft. She gathers up the last little fragments of chips and pushes them into her mouth. 'How come you know so much about it?'

I tell her I work in there, on maintenance, but I used to ride. She says do I mean horses, and I say no, rollercoasters.

'That's not a job,' she says.

'What's yours,' I ask her, 'Rent-a-mob?'

She drops the chip tray into a litter-bin and wipes her fingers on her big coat. 'I'm a volunteer,' she says. 'Captive Animals Protection Society. When was the last time you went the other side of that fence?'

'You can see from the top of the ride,' I say. 'Sort of grey tigers.'

'They're snow leopards,' she says sharply. 'They come from the mountains of central Asia, some of the wildest terrain on earth. And they're trapped right under your precious big dipper.'

I tell her it's not a big dipper, it's a coaster. One of the most famous classic woodies in Europe.

She snorts.

A few days later I see her again, on my side of the fence this time. On the bench by King Solomon's Mines, with a book open on her lap. She squints up at me in the sunshine and says 'Hey, it's the Rollercoaster Cowboy.'

I try not to look too delighted. I offer to show her the Cyclone, since she's shown an interest. She makes a face. Still, she snaps the book shut and puts it in her rucksack. I feel the no-mark lad on the Dodgems staring as I stroll by with this out-of-the-ordinary woman. With a woman.

'It looks a bit ramshackle compared with that one,' she says, nodding at the Traumatizer.

'Oh, that,' I say. 'Modern rubbish. Fur coat and no knickers.' I turn away and pretend to cough. What possessed me to use that word? 'Fancy a ride then?' Bloody hell, everything's coming out wrong.

She tells me she doesn't usually go on these things, she's not great with heights. Still, it's not exactly white-knuckle, is it? She climbs in and makes a big deal about the safety bar. Her nervousness makes her fiercer than ever, and when I lean across to demonstrate that it's securely locked she snaps: 'All right, keep your hands to yourself.'

I hardly notice the up and down or the fast and slow these days, just clench my jaw against the pain that rattles up through my spine. I steal a look at her face. Her eyes are wide and glittering. She doesn't scream. And actually her knuckles really are white against the red of the safety bar.

Afterwards, we walk down to the Elvis Café under the pier, and I tell her all about the record. What it was like going round and round that same little figure-of-eight track for twelve days and twelve nights. That's seventeen thousand two hundred and eighty minutes, I say. Or one million thirty-six thousand eight hundred seconds. She seems impressed. I tell her how boring it got, how I started feeling I was living inside my head, my body just a collection of aches and frustrations I happened to have attached to me. How the one thing that changed was the view, because sometimes the sea was a grey line in the far distance, and the beach was vast and empty, and sometimes the tide was in and there was a stiff wind frothing up a few waves and then it looked like proper seaside. I tell her how when it was over, I sat shivering among the empty cars all night, and at dawn I watched the fairground grow out of the mist – the Haunted House, the Waltzers, the River Caves – like a holy city (I actually use the words 'holy city', and she doesn't laugh either). I tell her that all I wanted then was an armchair and a plate of hot food. So I staggered home and got my mum out of bed and she cooked for me. But I rolled like a drunk, the chair pitched, the pie and potatoes wallowed about in my belly. It was like living in two countries, I tell her, and belonging in neither.

(I don't talk about the other stuff: the local radio, the pictures in *First Drop* and *Fairground Ephemera*, the trackwalks I lead for coaster clubs, the bloke who paid me a hundred quid to climb onto his girlfriend's car and propose to her in

33

rhyming couplets. It lacks the glamour.)

She goes and asks me about the world record, so I have to tell her how some American's just done eighty-three days. Not on a woodie, of course. And it was soft stuff: they built him a special carriage lined with rubber cushions and covered with canvas. Cheating sod.

We leave the café and cross the bridge over the Marine Lake, and she talks about snow leopards. There are only a few thousand left in the wild, she says, they could be extinct soon. The answer is to stop the fur trade, not keep them in zoos. Zoos are cruel and outdated. What do I think it's like for these shy, solitary creatures, caged next to a fairground, with the Cyclone rattling overhead every four minutes ten hours a day?

We meet once or twice a week after that. At first we ride the Cyclone, but after a few goes she starts to get used to it, and it's not so much fun then. So we go to the cafe, walk round the lake, or sit by the Ghost Train watching the punters. We have some good conversations, and sometimes we just sit there without talking at all. There's nothing physical between us yet, nothing at all, but I know you have to wait 'til the moment's right for all that. Women don't like to be rushed.

Operates a failsafe chain ascent, then gravity takes over – the more people on board, the faster it goes! Features a magic-eye brake warning system and three manual sets of brakes.

I'm spent up, bar the price of a pint. Time for a modest celebration. Back through the arcade, where all the world's losers are staring open-mouthed at screens, firing toy guns and picking their noses. There's a muddle of wet footprints near the door. Wet footprints? Christ, it's raining – a fucking downpour, would you believe it? I run, heading not for the pub but for Pleasureland. Fumble the padlock on the back gate and make for the Cyclone, but I know it already: the fire's out. The station's a mess, but the coaster itself's intact, just a bit blackened in places.

Fuck it. The rain runs off my jacket and soaks my boots. I can't even do this.

Loved by coaster enthusiasts the world over for its ingenious layout, traditional woodie thrills and its generosity with airtime…

The mug trembles in my hand and I take a big swig of scalding tea to try and steady myself.

'Where?' I manage to ask.

She sweeps the plastic table with a finger, gathering spilt sugar into a little drift.

'America,' she says, very definite. 'Upstate New York. I've got a placement with the Environmental Protection Agency. You remember I told you I'd applied.'

I rub my head. I don't remember at all. 'I'll come with you.'

Her finger stops very still above the sugardrift.

'There's another Cyclone there,' I jabber, 'at Coney Island. Eighty-five foot high. It can hit sixty mile an hour.'

A long silence. She thumbs the sugar flat.

'You're a great character.' Her voice is gentle. Christ, she feels sorry for me! 'But it's not like that, you know it isn't.'

'It could be…'

'No. No, it couldn't.'

It's very hot in here, it reeks of old dischcloths. I reach for her hand, but she twitches it away. The bench squeaks abruptly as she jumps to her feet.

…– that queasy weightless feeling that only a wooden coaster can give. Drops 3, 5 and 7 are the ones to watch!

I leave the gate swinging in the rain. I stumble into the park, walk the dripping corridors between privet hedges. I cut under the pier, escape into the anonymity of Ocean Plaza. Fast food and cheap shops – I could be anywhere. I start to feel stronger.

I cross the Coast Road, take the steps over the sea wall onto the beach. The sand creaks underfoot. Which way, Coral? *Coral.* A name with the sea in it. A foreign sea: warm and tropical, clear as air, alive with rainbow-coloured fish. Across the empty bay, the lights of Blackpool shiver in the rain. I'll walk and meet them.

Blue Guitar

Wish you were here. Now.

The wind and the sun. Marram-grass whipping at my legs. An impossible gradient of deep, soft sand.

It's the highest dune on this stretch of coast. Big Balls Hill, they call it – it's actually marked on the map. We used to laugh about it every time.

Of course you are here, in a way. When I brought you here that last time I thought I'd never feel lonely in this place. But it's not so easy. I come back every day and search. I dig with my hands, sieve the sand through my fingers, looking for you.

Sand. Treacherous stuff. Every couple of years someone stumbles across a corpse, bloated and stinking. Mostly suicides, washed up on a high tide. Now and then a murder. But it's the stupidest place to dispose of a body. The dunes shrug and shiver; the sand shifts, it's alive. A year, two years later, there's an arm sticking out of the sand for someone's dog to sniff at.

Or what's left of an arm.

But people do strike lucky, make incredible discoveries. There's that story – I'd like to believe in it – about a boy, playing at the edge of the sea, who found a wedding-ring. He took it to show his mother, and it turned out to be hers, which she'd lost there twenty years before. It's that kind of magic that keeps me going.

I'm not digging deep, just crawling along, skimming off the top layer and sifting it, skimming and sifting.

Sometimes I stop and look at a handful, and I see what a fool's errand this is. It's not one thing at all, it's a handful of different colours – more shades of white and brown and black than I could have guessed at.

Then I run, like something out of a cartoon, my legs pounding away at the slope but going nowhere fast. Collapse at the top, lie on my back watching the sky, with my heart pounding and the breath scalding my throat.

You used to love coming here, in both senses of the word. 'Race you down!'

We were always very competitive. But it was pure joy, leaping off the edge and then running, almost too fast for my feet, almost losing them, hurtling down into the soft bowl between hills, where it didn't matter if you fell, where it was safe. You at my back, grabbing my T-shirt and yanking me to the ground. The weight of you knocking the air out of my chest. You tugging at the stuck zip of my jeans and –

Christ, just thinking of it, the aching again, in all the usual places and spreading, up from the small of my back, along my spine, between my shoulder-blades…

I close my eyes against the dazzling sky. *Wish you were here.*

'Mrs Shaw?'

A woman in a tight suit was handing me something wrapped in brown paper.

'What? No.' My voice was too loud for the hush of the relatives' lounge. 'We weren't married. He didn't believe in it. We didn't believe in it.'

It was surprisingly light, I nearly dropped it. It was like a Christmas present or something. I tore it open there and then, pulled out a jar made of tinted plastic, with a gold-coloured screw lid. I held it up to the window and shook gently. Not much more than half-full.

The woman in the suit was staring. At the brown paper, discarded on the swirly nylon carpet. And at me.

'I'm so sorry,' she said.

Whatever I was expecting, it wasn't this. You hated plastic. Wouldn't buy bottled water because of the plastic. Because it's not biodegradable, it just sits there in the landfill with all the disposable nappies and other shit for ever and ever. In the van, we had a piece of smoothed and oiled sycamore for a chopping-board, we bought our apple juice in glass bottles which we refilled at the healthfood shop for twice the supermarket price. We used a slightly mildewed wicker basket for the washing. We collected driftwood sculptures on the beach for the wood-burning stove; they took weeks to dry out, filled the van with a salty, foreign smell.

It wasn't as if you'd left instructions. The illness was too fast. In those last days you surprised me, didn't want to face what was coming. I was too much of a coward to bring it up. I took my lead from you, and from the relentlessly bright atmosphere of the hospital ward, nurses jollying the patients along as if it was a holiday camp. I'd have expected you to loathe every minute of that, but you went for it, the banter and the smiles. I sat beside the bed like a boring old aunt at a party. You were dying – every day your face was thinner and greyer – and all you wanted to do was joke with the porter.

'Off for a smoke? Have one for me, mate. And put something extra in it, know what I mean?'

So I never asked you any of those questions: what music you wanted at your funeral, what I should do with the ashes. You might have laughed, or cried, and I couldn't have stood either. So I made the decisions. There would be no funeral. No one would have come anyway.

Back at the van, I opened the jar, pinched a bit of the dust between my fingers and sniffed cautiously. Its faint scent reminded me of a cupboard I hid in once as a child, during a game of hide-and-seek when no one came to find me. Funny, I thought I'd be squeamish, but it was remarkably clean stuff, nothing to be afraid of. Hard to believe a human body could be reduced to such small volume. Especially your body, with its beautiful complications, its fierce impulses. I put on your donkey-jacket, tucked the jar inside it, slogged up Big Balls Hill and sowed you like seed on the wind.

It was embarrassing, if you want to know the truth. No one else seemed to notice – the dog-walkers, the joggers, the lovers – but I was embarrassed in front of myself. It's a melodramatic gesture, scattering someone's ashes. Perhaps I should say a few words? A poem? A prayer even?

But you hated ceremony of any kind, and anyway you were *dead*.

I tried not to watch myself unscrewing the lid and shaking the jar, the ashes snatched on the air, like dust off the old rag-rug when I shake it outside the van.

And the plastic jar? The least I could do was dispose of it thoughtfully, as it says on crisp packets. I dropped it in the bin by the information point, forcing myself to pause and pretend to read about the unusual breeding habits of the natterjack toad.

Then I went home.

'Houses are too permanent,' you said, as we walked along a road of semis and bungalows, passing at least half a dozen For Sale signs. 'Get a house and you start buying stuff – washing machine, carpets, lawnmower…' You made them sound like the devil's trinkets. 'You ever helped anyone move house? They have stuff in the attic, stuff in the cellar, they're clogged up with stuff like arteries clogged up with fat… that's unrestrained fucking capitalism for you.'

In theory we could have moved house whenever we wanted, gone on the road, if we'd got the brakes seen to first. But we didn't bother. It was OK here, at the back of the caravan site. We only paid a couple of hundred a year, a friend of a friend. It was quiet. We were busy staying in bed, keeping warm. There was the daily walk to the sand-dunes. And I wrote the odd piece for women's magazines – *Is There*

Life After 35? and *20 Ways to Say No to your Boss* – while you sprawled on the bench, singing and playing your blue guitar.

By the way, the guitar went with you. It was the only thing you had that was truly yours. I took it out behind the van, stuffed it with paper and set light to it. It didn't burn very well. A smell of scorched varnish, and a surprising amount of metal and plastic. I scraped up the ashes with a tablespoon and added them to the jar, shook it all up together. Now you were all mixed up with little scraps of unburnt wood and bits of grass.

'What's it gonna be, babe?'

When you were playing guitar your voice changed, you acquired a West Coast drawl. You could play for hours, Dylan to Dire Straits. Sometimes it was as if you couldn't stop.

'Don't call me babe.'

You took a long ecstatic pull on your joint and stuck it between the strings and the fret.

'Lay lady, lay, lay across my big brass bed…'

'Not that, you know I hate it.'

The van was sleepy and stoned. I rubbed my eyes and turned back to the glare of the laptop.

'Stay lady stay, stay with your man awhile…'

'Stop it, I mean it now. Unless you want me to throw up.'

'Why? Why doncha like it?'

'You know why. I told you.' I really did feel queasy.

'Tell me again, babe. What happened to you all those long years ago? C'mon now, tell Daddy all about it.'

'Shut up.'

'His clothes are dirty but his hands are clean…'

'You bastard!' I dived across the van, dashed the guitar from your hands to the floor with a splintering wrong chord. For a few seconds we just stared at each other. I watched your face, ready to fling myself at the door and escape.

'We're on fucking fire!' You sprang off the bench and

stamped on the smouldering joint, the tiny hole in the rug. Then you pulled me down with you and we were laughing and wrestling, jostling strange music from the loose guitar. The bench and the cupboard rolled us back and forth like a ship's cabin in a storm. You had a way of touching, very sure and exact…

…but I don't want to think about that. The aching, the wanting, it gets into my bones. I'm cold and tired of searching.

And what's the point? I know where you are. Everywhere, very finely scattered.

Right here, where I'm lying, at the foot of Big Balls Hill.

I just need to feel you on my skin. The jacket's going to have to come off. And the jeans, though it's freezing in this wind. I'm going to pull them off quick and businesslike, not think of you easing them over my hips, not think of your grin.

That's good. Scooping sand all over myself. There's bound to be some of you in there.

And here comes the rain, which makes it even better. You're plastered to my arms and legs and stomach, and I'm feeling warmer already.

TIM COOKE

The Priest

There's someone on the stairs again, the bloke from downstairs, The Priest, playing his pan pipe. I'm stuck in the black lift of my depression as always, falling through the floors with dizzying speed, but I edge out along the hallway anyway, parting the darkness as I go, and look through the spyhole to make sure it's him. He's not visible but there's something about the random, automatic quality of the playing, the pointlessness of it, that tells me it's him. As I crouch down and listen to the squealing mess of sound pressing under the door, I feel, not for the first time, as if I'm under attack.

A week ago he was out on the estate cursing at three in the morning:

'Your fucking IRA, your CIA, your CID, your tenants' association, your fucking middle-class urban decay junkies, your cat-lovers, I fucking hate you all, you cunting tourists.'

The tirade went on for two hours during which he managed to castigate, with some originality, almost the nameable itself. Two years ago I would have gone down and had a word with him, talked him out of it, laid a reassuring arm upon his shoulder, but now that I have lost my mind, now that buying a pint of milk is near the limit of my capability, all I can do is listen, mortuarised in bed, staring at the cracked and faded white of the ceiling, and wait for his psychosis to burn itself out. My worst fear as the list mushroomed beyond plausibility was that there was method to it, that it was a form of divining and that he was seeking amongst his lexicon for the source of all his pain and anger, his true enemy. I found myself mouthing the words for which he was searching and thinking with mounting horror that I had reached them only a second ahead of him and that as soon as they were reiterated by his own lips he would turn to the window and then hurtle up the stairs and hammer on the door, the awful crowd of his madness streaming behind him.

But the moment passed and the multiplication of paranoias was averted. In fact the final object of his derision was a yoghurt pot he found attached to his trousers after falling off the stolen car-parking sign upon which he'd been precariously balancing. This I observed guiltily, my chin pressed to the window-sill, before watching him disappear through the door directly beneath me. There was the slurring of feet, then nothing. The sign swung unsteadily for a few moments more, seeming briefly almost animate against the dark grass, then as if suddenly reacquainted with its own futility, ground abruptly to a halt. In the distance I could hear the Mancunian Way and Princess Parkway across the mouldering rooftops and it sounded like bliss.

Some days I don't hear a peep out of him. True, there is the stench as I pass by his door, which I guess counts as some sort of contact, and always some new graffiti or scrawling, the latest being, improbably, a backstage door sticker for a girl band called the Sugababes. This level of interaction suits me fine. Then there's just me to deal with, dragging my lifeless form through the dreary rooms of my first-floor mausoleum where months can go by without a single object moving, apart from the two plates, cutlery and mug that shuttle between the living room and the washing-up bowl. Everything is exactly as it was two years ago, as if I'd died back then and have been living on in memory only. The dust is that thick, all the plants are dead, and the walls are hung with shabby items of clothing from more glorious times. Two years ago I thought I had completely lost my self. Now I realised that I had lost even that loss. In such a situation, when you can no longer see the big picture because you are no longer part of it, details are everything, details are all there is left.

Two years ago nothing happened. Nothing really anyway. My housemate went away, returned to Vancouver. True, he felt like a soul-mate and losing him was like letting go of the best part of myself, but at the time I felt quite powerful, magus-like, and we had fallen out somewhat and I thought it'd be best for both of us. But what moves in when the best part of yourself moves out? Can a man die because he loses a friend? Looking at the minutiae of the situation, the detail that strikes me is that he took my guitar cord instead of his, mine with the brand-name Piranha clearly marked in white on black rather than his own which had no label. Did he do that out of affection, because he wanted something to remember me by? No, because he already had several more appropriate items. Or was it a simple mistake: he just grabbed the wrong cord in the hurry to get packed? Unlikely, he was very precious about all of his music gear. So why? What did the cord signify? I stared blankly out of the window at the grey, morbid sky that seemed to hang permanently over Hulme Park in the unlikely hope of finding solace.

The cord connected my Fender bass to its Trace Elliot amplifier. So did it earth me, ground me in some way? Was it my connection that he took, that he coveted and wanted for himself? Who was he anyway, this Canadian who appeared from nowhere and moved into this flat within a few days of me arriving myself? Who became so quickly such a close friend, whose music sounded from the first so delightful, so natural, so perfect, as if I had heard it all before? More than that, I thought with a start, as if I had written it myself, as if it was somehow my music too.

From the stairwell, as if by way of sardonic commentary, a guitar started to strum tunelessly. A guitar now! Fuck. That meant I was imprisoned for the next couple of hours unless I fancied trying to get past him on the stairs. This was no easy task since The Priest always sprawled across the landing, effectively barricading the way, and moved to block you if you tried to go around him. At the same time, he would be staring with unseeing eyes at some insignificant scrap of nothingness on the wall and acting for all the world as if he were in some sort of deep trance or meditation rendering him incapable of speech or understanding. Whether this was a real manifestation of his illness, a consequence of his medication, or an affectation, I didn't know. Maybe it was all three. But it was certainly unnerving, the sort of challenge that you didn't need when your head was fit to explode with self-doubt and foreboding and you were having problems going to the shops.

I turned on the TV and tried to drown out the sound but he had started singing now and it was impossible not to listen. I was fairly sure that he just made the lyrics up as he went along – they certainly never sounded as if they'd been crafted in any way or honed to work with a consistent theme or even with each other. It was just the cursing in the night by other means as far as I was concerned. One of his favourite tricks was to repeat the same word over and over again whilst playing a two- or three-chord sequence. Today the word seemed like it was 'dislocation'. This could go on for an hour without the slightest variation, following which there might be a slight shift in emphasis to something like 'I'm dislocating' or a verbal pun such as 'in dis location'. It was agonising, especially to me since he seemed to have precisely the ability to be in the present that I lacked. For whilst it's true that I sat in my flat and, generally speaking, did nothing because my brain was so messed up that I couldn't work or socialise or even read, this was more because I was so overwhelmed by the total fuck-up that was my past and the anxiety that this generated than because of anything actually happening in the present or likely to happen in the future. My mind seemed to have ganged up on itself and was in the process of eradicating any connection that it had with reality, even with itself. Shit, there was that word again – connection. Wait. Hougen had taken my connection because I was so intent on losing it myself, because he was sick of it, wanted me to see what I was doing to myself. My better half took my connection with reality because he was that connection i.e. he effectively took himself!

I stood up and started pacing around the room, my head in my hands, my eyes darting between the dilapidated mismatched sofas, the wooden pallet covered in badly arranged bits and pieces – candle-holders without candles, empty room fragrance bottles, a stripey sausage-dog face down in the dirt – the browning remains of the dragon tree in the corner, the numerous worn-out pairs of shoes on the floor. Incoherent fragments, shards of a life, signifiers of ruin. I went over to the mirror and gazed desperately at the face I no longer recognised as mine.

The Priest was really getting going now. The words had changed and I strained to hear them. I'm always nervous of going to the door because I'm sure either that he can hear me, or that his psychosis grants him supernatural powers and he can sense my encroachment, my presence, my auditory voyeurism. So I stood by the door to the lounge and inclined my ear in his direction. He was doing an exaggerated Radiohead impression with plenty of phlegm and the mantra he was cycling through like Thom Yorke on opium was:

'You're disconnected, yeah, you're disconnected.'

Everything in its right place. Maybe there were no accidents, everything was scripted, all the world a stage, though not a divine authority but instead a sort of evil genius. Or perhaps you oscillated between the two like a pendulum, divine authority/evil genius according to some sort of magnetic orientation, the way you were facing at the time. Look down and all you see is hell, look up and there's only heaven. I began to get a very bad feeling about The Priest. I had lost faith in Hougen, that was the truth of it, I had stopped believing in him. I thought I could survive without him. As a result, he had left and taken my guitar cord with him and since then I had been falling non-stop, indeed I no longer felt like I existed. A reasonable period of time had been allowed to elapse and then The Priest had arrived. The black lift I was travelling in had stopped at his floor and he had got in.

A distorted version of Hougen, like a reflection in a trick-mirror at a fairground, he looked like a movie-maker's idea of an asylum inmate. Shaved head, glaucous unfocused eyes, twisted grin, pasty dough-like skin, menacing mien and clothing presumably from a skip – though he was undoubtedly capable of intelligent thought, he concealed it well. Where Hougen was musically adept and generally astute, the only reasoned communication I had had with The Priest was when he knocked at my door and asked me if I could teach him scales on the piano. Where I had welcomed Hougen into my flat and given him a room for two years, loving his genial sort of madness, I squirmed away from any contact with The Priest, telling him that I was too fucked up, too doped with anti-depressants to teach anyone anything. Since then we had nodded at each other a few times, grunted to say hello but our communications have been strictly Early Man.

For months now I have seen him as nothing more than a nuisance, an irritation that I can't scratch, an encumbrance like a scab or a tumour that has attached itself to my block of flats. Most of the time I have not looked, I have ignored, I have stepped over and passed by but for someone so confined, I should have realised that there is more at stake in such a person coming to live in my block. I should have seen him in relation to Hougen. I should have put him in context. I should have seen him as a motivated sign and not been taken in by the apparent Brownian motion of his behaviour.

I went into the kitchen and started the kettle boiling to make a coffee, realising that it was two hours since I'd started this latest reverie about Hougen. The Priest was humming now, much quieter, stroking the guitar as if he was gradually passing out. Sometimes when he stopped playing he just lay there, which meant you never knew for sure whether he was still on the stairs or not until you opened the door. It seemed like he was heading that way now. I wondered who he actually was. Where he came from. Why he was called The Priest, for fuck's sake? Though things with him had begun slowly, in the colon as it were, the recent metastatic proliferation made it difficult to understand why I had never asked any of these questions before. Why was I so scrupulously not interested in him? It began to look like a psychological strategy, not so much repression but more what I remembered Freud calling 'foreclosure', treating something as if it did not exist, a technique reserved for true horrors. But how could I find out more about him? I looked in the fridge and found that I'd run out of milk. 'Screw your courage to the sticking point', I thought. There was no avoiding it – I would have to go out.

The boiling of the kettle had momentarily drowned out the sounds from the hallway and now, as I listened, I realised they had completely died away. Gone or comatose, I had to find out. Putting on my coat, I eased the door open a crack and gingerly stuck my head out. There was no sign of him. I shut the door behind me, locked it and made my way towards the stairs feeling as if clouds had suddenly given way to clear sky. True, he may be waiting at his door to loom out at me as he often did, but I could brush my way past that with a cursory 'hiya'. I hurried down, intent on getting out of the building as quickly as I could, determined not to give his doorway even a glance, but as I passed it I sensed that something was not quite right and looked around. I had evidently felt a draught or some sort of emptiness emanating from the flat, because when I turned I saw that there was no door in the doorway. It had completely disappeared. More madness, I thought. He's removed his own door in an attempt to get back to an even more primal stage of development. I pulled back, imagining him coming at me with a club, clothed in animal skins, his face camouflaged with excrement. For a second I fancied I saw him in the darkness but it was just my own mind projecting ahead, plaguing me once again.

More to quell my own fear than out of curiosity or concern, I called out:

'Priest? Priest? Are you in there?'

The words span into the mouth of the flat like stones, ricocheting harshly. But though the darkness seemed to have a presence and certainly possessed quite an odour, neither were sufficient to make me believe the flat currently contained anything particularly animate and, without really knowing what I was doing, somehow impelled by the situation, I found myself crossing the threshold. I tried the light switch. Nothing. No bulb or no power. I took another step, or rather slid along like a cadaver entering a furnace. I knew the layout of the flat – it was the mirror of mine so all I had to do was think in reverse. Down at the bottom of the hallway was the sitting room. That's where I would head first. Now that I was in there, in the guts of his abode and with a legitimate excuse, I was intrigued as to what I might find. Perhaps I could answer some of the questions, find out who he really was, what he was about. I knew I might not have much time, so I made the lounge as quickly as I could, stumbling over unseen debris, and scraped down the wall where I knew the light switch ought to be. It was there, and this time the light came on, although it was a red bulb and made me feel as if my eyes had suddenly switched to infrared.

I looked around me, swivelled my eyes here and there, trying to pick up some information quickly. The floor was carpeted with clothes; I had felt that with my feet but now I could see them, dozens of garments but no actual carpet beneath them, just cold concrete. To the left there was an old and seemingly melted computer, like something out of Dali, every part of it seemed to be burned and mis-shapen. Grotesque though it was, it was the same model as my own, an Apple, so he had had taste – and money – once. By the side of it there was a stack of handwritten sheets, a book of some sort perhaps, since I found it hard to believe he could still be a student. However the top sheet had the word 'shit' scrawled across it in what looked like blood or something worse. By the window there was a television or what remained of one: the tube was smashed and a broom handle was sticking out of it. To the right there was an immense mound of objects that, out of the corner of my eye, in the carnadine, made me think of cows piled up, a great pyre. Books, and beneath them records – singles and albums. Masses of them. I bent down and picked up a handful of paperbacks. In the gloom I could just make out the covers and some of the titles: 'The Nature of Things', 'Seven Clues to the Origins of Life', 'The Postcard', 'Four Fundamental Concepts'. I started slightly, somewhat bemused. These were all books that I'd read, that I'd once possessed. I grabbed another handful: Barthes' 'S/Z', a Haruki Murakami, 'The Theory and Practice of Hypnotism', an A to Z of Brighton. Ridiculous, these were all mine too – and much more unlikely. I fell onto my knees and ploughed into the barrow, hunting for vinyl now: The Pale Saints, Slowdive, Dif Juz, Bauhaus, a staggeringly rare Josef K single. Every time my hand came up, it was with a record or a book that I had not only once known but that had previously been mine. Crazy. I delved again and again but there were no exceptions. Not a single aberration from that rule, and I searched and I searched through what must have been well over a thousand objects, tumbling the mountain down around me.

By the end I was drained, almost diseased, and felt like I was losing my mind all over again. It was impossible but there it was. All of the precious belongings that a bitter ex-girlfriend had once given away to charity because I hadn't been able to pick them up on an allotted day, they were all here. In The Priest's flat. The whole of my book and vinyl collection built up over thirty years. What, had she given them all somehow directly to him? Were these actually my things, or was this just some sort of carbon copy of my own unique journey, a continuation across dimensions of a chaotic logic? I scrabbled around to see if I could find an inscription, a name in any of the frontispieces or on the sleeves but came up with nothing. They probably weren't mine then, I thought, slightly relieved, but that didn't make the situation much better. Was I really supposed to believe that The Priest had read all of those texts? Tracked down all of those singles and EPs? That he had, by himself, without aid of any kind, built up such an esoteric collection? That he was that sort of guy? But then I'd amassed them in the first place, and what sort of a guy was I now?

I realised I had to get out of there. I was losing my grip and if he walked in now I didn't think I could cope, would probably just fall to pieces and start yelling – which might lead to anything. But as I left I couldn't prevent myself from glancing quickly into the bedroom – my bed, the same make, a Panasonic hi-fi, ditto – and the kitchen – an old Moffat stove like mine – enough to realise that The Priest's flat was like a hellish vision of my own, maybe ten years down the line, that he in some sense was me, that the universe was mocking me once again, playing a sick joke on my naivety, balancing out some sort of dreadful equation for my benefit. I wasn't who I thought I was. No one was. We were all just parts of something, heads on a single, bifurcated body, bound together by the same deep structure that could show you the good side or the bad side of itself depending on the decisions you made, the people you loved, the people you rejected, the direction you took. I knew which side I was being shown and I felt like Scrooge after the vision of Christmas future, only truly damned.

When I got back into my own flat, I slammed the door, locked it and then slid down it onto the floor. If The Priest was me, or some part or version of me, and he'd been moved into these flats because of his relation to me, then who was everyone else? Carlos on the top floor, Elaine, Michelle downstairs, Thomas opposite? The only one I ever talked to now was Thomas and even he'd stopped borrowing tobacco like he used to or giving me plants, and talked to me in that patronising, slow way people use for those they believe have lost it. I realised that over the past two years I'd stopped talking to everyone on the estate, many of whom I used to count as friends. If they are all part of me, if I am somehow living inside my own mind, then I am becoming a particle in an environment that abhors the particulate, a single neurone disconnected from the net. Suddenly, behind me, underneath the door, I hear what sounds like a dog sniffing.

I jump up, startled. A dog? Then I realise that the dog is enunciating something: not quite words, but not animal sounds either. A grinding, guttural monotone. Horrified, I run into the bedroom and shut the door. I turn on the light but the bulb explodes and the darkness caves in around me and something like dynamite goes off inside my head. I am panicking badly, have to control my breathing. If all the people in this block are in some sense here for me, feel me, sense my disconnection from them, then what about everyone on the estate? This peculiar, road-locked, ramshackle, paralysed estate on the shoreline of the city centre? Is this why I beached up here? A place that is literally at the end of all roads? What will happen now that I have seen the books, the records, the flat, now that I realise what is really going on?

I grope my way towards the window, desperate for air, and look out onto the avenue. At first I think that something has happened to the grass below, that it has become somehow lumpen, goose-fleshed, horripilated but then, gradually, like a magic-eye picture, I resolve the image. There are hundreds of people standing on the grass, in the darkness, staring up at me. The strange effect is made by all their heads together so unexpectedly. Their eyes glitter dully like felspar in granite. I blink in refusal, cast about wildly for the car parking sign only to find that it has disappeared, swallowed up by the heave of bodies whose mute ceremony slowly forces itself upon me. It is incredible. From the numbers it appears that the whole of the estate has turned out for reasons that both appal and are beyond me, and as I stand transfixed I have the vertiginous sensation that the floor beneath me, the very earth, is slipping away. Such a crowd, such a mass. So many people I have ignored and let slip by. But where is he? Where is The Priest?

Behind me there is the click of the door opening. I half-turn. The black lift has stopped at the basement, and they are waiting for me to get out.

The Letter K

They called him Finn because his hair was red and he reminded someone, some time of a story they'd read about the Irish hero Finn MacCool. It wasn't his real name.

'I am not who I am, ha ha,' he typed and on the screen the words unfurled fitfully, looking, it seemed to him, like nothing so much as an emergent colony of insects walking on a white tightrope. He found himself thinking about the Cambrian explosion, the Burgess Shale and all the bizarre never-to-be-repeated designs it had thrown up: insects with odd numbers of legs, insects with no apparent symmetry, insects that rolled around on wheels. Had he dreamt that last one? He deleted the text before anyone noticed it, turned away from the monitor and gazed past the potted fig through the treble-glazed window. The sun was ragged and somehow misshapen and the sky draped like an empty house and he fancied he could almost hear a high-pitched keening that it took him some moments to place as actually coming from somewhere underneath the table. Ah, the router was playing up again. Time for a break from the remorseless digital pitter-patter, from the branding of white mythological flesh, from the opening of portals onto the single black hole that underlay every innocent page.

Upstairs in the dubiously-titled 'Recreation Area' (dubious he thought because it was styled so deliberately in the manner of a waiting room that creation or relaxation were the last things likely to happen there), Finn stirred himself a coffee and sat down on the formless sofa, managing as he did so to spill a little of the spume from the coffee onto the aridity that was the table. Okay, so he was forty-one and he was a typist, had been a typist these last seven years and had singularly failed to move on, even from this one department. Before that he had been an English lecturer, a head of department, filled with ambition. But then something had happened. Something serious. These were the facts. He idled a pencil inside the mug, trying to dredge up the raw cane sugar at the bottom.

Some said he had gone mad, lost his marbles, descended into some sort of psychotic hinterland for a year or so and never managed to fully climb back. Others, his doctor among them, were of the opinion that it was some sort of personality disorder, a degenerative condition that had finally rendered him too conscious, a left brainer without the depth, intuition and balance of the right, a burnt-out fire. To Finn it was simple: he had gained the world for a moment but then in retribution he had lost his soul. However, once, somewhere in the middle of the process, albeit for a short time, he had been in paradise. *Et in Arcadia ego*, he mused as he drew finally on the coffee. He was still intelligent. It was just that he had no desire, no will, no purpose any more.

Outside, impossibly, there was the sound of a bird cawing. A crow or a rook, but no, this was the forty-second floor, and there was always the glazing. He angled his head to locate the source and sideswiped his eyes: an open window, narrow, by the sink. It was the first time he'd ever seen such a thing in the building. As far as he was aware, there were no windows that opened, the building was hermetically sealed since, as it said in the Starters' Manual 'the air-conditioning precluded any such need.' But there it was. Had it always been there? Coffee in hand, he stood up and went to take a look. Okay, the frame was a white sort of PVC like all the others, but never mind triple-glazed, this one wasn't even double-glazed and it had a handle. He craned his head out of it and the crow or rook cawed again, though this time it was more of a long 'caaaaaa' but for the life of him he couldn't catch a glimpse of it.

After a few minutes of useless neck-twisting he pulled his head in, drank in a breath or two of the cool, fresh air and then returned to the table, leaving the window ajar. As he sat, two thoughts crossed his mind. One, that this was the first genuinely curious thing that had happened to him since he'd started with the Bureau, though there'd been a concatenation before that. Two, that by tomorrow, perhaps, the window would have returned to normal or even – he shunned this slightly from his mind – wouldn't be there at all. For this reason, perhaps, when his break ended, he found himself unusually reluctant to leave.

The next day began like any other. Radio, cereal, newspaper, coffee, tram, work. As normal, he forced himself not to have a cigarette until an hour after he'd woken up, and as normal he spluttered as he inhaled the first drag. The only thing he positively noticed on the journey in was that an entire building, twenty or so storeys of it, had been somehow coated overnight in an advertisement for the Ford Ka. Walking along the opposing pavement on the way up to Piccadilly, it seemed as if you were permanently on the verge of being run down and crushed like a bug by the vehicle, and Finn found it hard to see how anyone would find this thought appealing. As he passed by, coincidentally perhaps though he didn't give it much of a thought, there was the staccato sound of an engine misstarting, a 'kakaka' that if he had converted it into phonetics might have made him think of Samuel Beckett and excrement.

When he finally spilled into the office from the lift, it was to find the women (it was an all-female office bar him) milling around a box containing a cake of some description and a pile of unfamiliar purple folders on his desk. Fuck, what was this all about? He felt as if he was growing taller, more obvious somehow, and his eyes seemed to pull focus on the room so that everyone moved away whilst worryingly remaining the same size. He stumbled, sweat prickling on his forehead as he tried to make conversation with Liz and Jennie, his usual talk-mates and he couldn't help flicking his eyes as he talked over the other nine workstations searching for any hints of purple in the otherwise uniform manila stacks. There were none. He felt sick.

'Finn, you alright? You look a bit strung out. You coming down with something?'

Two changes in two days. Too much. Something was happening.

'Yeah, no I'm fine, Liz, just need some air or something. Too much pollution on the streets, maybe.'

They all moved in and were attentive, anything to break the monotony, and after a brief consultation he was sent to the Rec. Room. Relief at last. The window was still there, though shut now and, it appeared upon further examination, locked. Finn sat down and put his head in his hands. Purple folders. What could they mean? Another department sending down its business to the pool? But why only him? Why had he alone been shifted onto new work, and why hadn't he been warned? Why had the cake seemed so much more important than such a shattering change to his work regime, a regime established and unvaried over seven whole years? Maybe it was a trivial thing, though. Maybe they'd simply run out of the standard folders and had to use some spares. After all, he'd only seen the packaging – the contents could well be the same as always. A variation on the 'Same Shit, Different Day' motif.

But they weren't the same. The typing the office generally handled was always signed off 'DfS', which stood for the Department for Scrutiny though, since the documents were principally high-brow academic articles and rarefied abstracts, the acronym was more informally and secretively transliterated as 'Dead-end for Sense'. The documents Finn discovered in the purple folders were signed off 'K2' and as he sidled his way through them, he found them to be an eclectic and entirely perplexing mix. He looked around and, seeing that no one was paying any attention to him, that they were all rattling at their keyboards and chit-chattering as they would any Friday morning, he decided to take advantage of his appendix-like position in the room and spend the day reconnoitring the extent of this new, textual estrangement.

There were thirty-three texts in all. The first was a poem, something about the moon being more than it seemed, some sort of machine, an eyeball for another consciousness. It was anything but run-of-the-mill. The second was a garage receipt, a list of replacement parts for – he stuttered internally at this – a Ford Ka. The third was a long diatribe on, amongst other things, mind control, its author claiming to be someone called Koresh, a name Finn faintly remembered hearing but couldn't think where. The fourth was a short story, ten or twelve pages, called 'The Priest' about a man who's cracking up in a block of flats and who realises too late that the chap downstairs, the Priest of the title, is actually a distorted, degraded version of himself. The fifth, a song titled 'Loki', seemed to be written from the perspective of a paranoid secret agent and contained the lines:

They wanted me to shoot you, break your fall
They wanted someone else to make their call
They look through me, they don't see you at all
You are the sun at night, you want it all.

And so on, and so on. Finn felt as if he'd stepped through into another sort of reality, one in which he wasn't slowly dying, fading away to nothing beneath his own pitiless gaze, but instead was turned inside out and given something substantial to graze upon, a reality in which he could, perhaps, be alive. He couldn't help himself blinking as he opened each folder, so completely unexpected were its contents every time. It was hallucinogenic, there was no doubt about that, and he wondered if he'd somehow ingested some sort of drug. Maybe one of the vitamin pills he choked on every morning had contained something decidedly stranger than the ingredients claimed on the label. But no, that was ridiculous. The folders were clearly, empirically there; reality was as hard or as soft as it should objectively be. His body, the paper, the purr of the air-conditioning, the hum of the women around him, all were ... – but then he noticed that he couldn't actually hear anyone talking. Well, no actual words anyway. There was suddenly just a language-like sound, as if you'd taken all the speech and put it in a linguistic washing machine to clean it of any distinguishable marks. Every so often he could hear a syllable or two, but it was more like a door catch or the sound of a latch clicking. Yes, like the clicks he'd heard in some African dialects at University, or the sound of insects hitting a light bulb. And the really odd thing was that, as he first found when he went to the toilet, the longer he was away from his desk and in particular the purple folders, the more the speech returned to normal whereas as soon as he immersed himself once more, so the washing machine effect took over with its strange, leaping clicks. It was almost amusing and for the rest of the morning he played with moving between the zones, outside and inside, using the excuse of his being a bit under the weather for his unusual level of isolation from the rest of the pool and the furious diligence of his typing.

By the end of the day, Finn had typed all thirty-three of the texts, printed them out, proofed them and then handed them over to Mary, the office manager, to send on. He was tempted to keep copies of some of the more intriguing ones but decided against it. For one thing, it was strictly forbidden to remove anything from the building, and for another, he'd simply never thought of taking anything out before and so lacked the expertise and preparation that would be necessary to pull it off. Added to this, he had the demeanour of a man who's just stepped off a roller-coaster for one, a unique brand of breathless wonder and confusion that made him feel as if his every action away from the texts would be the subject of intense scrutiny. As a result, he was unable even to ask his intended question about K2 and the destination of his day's work and it was all he could do to mumble:

'See you Monday,' and walk in a daze to the lift.

Saturday morning, and he was as confused as ever. Reading the papers didn't help either, and after an hour of perusing the same miserable paragraphs over and over again, he threw them to the floor and put his head in his hands. There would be no relief, he knew, until he got a safe handle on things, found a rationale for the whole perplexing affair. On reviewing the events of the previous day, playing them back and forth before his mind's eye, Finn found himself feeling both irritated and a little frightened. He simply couldn't understand what had taken place. Yes, it had been exciting in a way, enthralling even, but why the hell had no one pointed the obvious fingers or asked the questions that pleaded to be asked. What's in the purple folders? Why have you been moved onto new work? What the fuck's going on? It wasn't as if there was only one, strikingly different folder, or as if he'd only been working on it for five minutes. In those circumstances, he could have understood them being too wrapped up in what they were doing to notice. But a whole day? A stack of folders that glared like a beacon?

It wasn't as if Jennie or Liz hadn't come over to him and chatted or asked for things (though he'd failed to grasp what they were talking about and had to rely on hand gestures when they wanted staplers or hole-punchers). Nor had they behaved as if they'd been prepared for it beforehand. As far as he could tell, they were their normal selves. It was more the case that they seemed utterly incapable of seeing that there was anything out of the ordinary going on, as if they were entirely blind to that to which they could not reasonably be blind. That was the crux of it, that was the conundrum. The folders and the arcane pieces of writing within them were for his eyes only and had been routed through the office, had made their journey in and out, as if they belonged to another dimension, as if rather than the folders being purple, they and their contents had been somehow coded in ultra-violet, off the visual scale. All at once he slammed his fist down on the coffee table, so hard that the ricochet jolted the radio into action. He just managed to hear the words '…musical cacophony' before he hit the off switch and returned to his incomprehension.

Something was trying to say itself, that much was sure. But was it a communication to him or from him? Inside or outside? Reality had got its wires crossed just as it had eight years before, and he had that same feeling again that he was being singled out for a performance to an audience of one. Even as he thought the words, two things did occur: somebody knocked hard on the door and rattled the letterbox, and Finn's cat La shot through the kitchen as if pursued by devils and bolted through the cat-flap. It is happening again, Finn thought and the certainty of the feeling both exhilarated and appalled him. Seven years of an existence only exponentially related to life and then, caboom. Strangeness. Thought and reality shading into each other, fusing, becoming one.

He pulled himself up and made for the front door, half-knowing what he would find but at the same time doubting it, uncertain as to whether it would be what it appeared to be or whether he was already constructing something out of nothing. Even as he approached the entrance hall, he could tell from the blurry uniformity of the dark figures muttering and kicking their heels in the porch that they were not anybody to whom he felt compelled to open the door.

Probably politicos or Jehovah's Witnesses, he thought and then changing heart suddenly stole behind the skeletal form of the old hatstand on the left in order to wait them out. He could hear from their tones that it was a man and a woman though he couldn't make out any actual words. Despite his concealment he felt peculiarly exposed, almost as if whoever they were, they were able to look through walls or around corners, to pry even into his rather gloomy recess. That said, a few minutes later he heard their voices become more abrupt and decisive. There was some scuffling and then something very thick was crushed into the letterbox, after which he was grateful to hear the footsteps on the concrete depart and gradually fade away to nothing. He waited for a few seconds more to be safe and then slid across and wrenched the wad from the door. On opening it up he saw, as he walked back into the kitchen, that it was some sort of religious tract, the font very Biblical and old world, although the terms in which it was couched were certainly not Christian.

'I should put it in the rubbish right now, without looking at it,' he said aloud to himself, knowing that he could back out here just as he could have refused to type the purple texts until he'd been given an explanation. But he knew that there was something about him that savoured uniqueness, that loved the idea that he was the target, set apart, that – dead or alive – he was the one.

So, though he agonised for a moment or two, his hand suspended over the bin, he slowly brought it up, unfolded it and began to read. It was as he thought, ridiculous – not random, a connecting text.

In the beginning were Ra and Gaia – what we now know as the Sun and the Earth, it began.

Finn thought of his cat and smiled. Who knows this stuff, he mused, then, after switching the kettle on to make another cafetiere, he returned to document, wondering whether it was the thirty-forth in the sequence.

The context of the article, if you could call it that, seemed to be ancient Egypt and it implied over and again that the mindset of the ancient Egyptians was collectively solipsistic in the sense that they, the author somehow presumed to know, both saw themselves as being a single individual divided into the two apparent agencies of male and female (rather as the body is 'divided' into left and right), while simultaneously thinking that that they were the point and purpose of reality itself, almost as if reality were the dream they were having. In this barely imaginable sense, they WERE the sun and earth, married and in perpetual embrace, a single body. The text flowed on at great length about what this meant: 'as above, so below,' a phrase Finn fancied he'd heard before, a group mind, telepathy, no need for words, empathic fusion, the pyramids not built but imagined, no concept of two, a sort of paradise, Adam and Eve and the later Serpent based on this. It was a species of eulogy written with a frightening intensity, written by somebody that you probably wouldn't want to meet on a dark night. The thought flickered in Finn's mind that maybe this sort of writing was itself a form of mind control, that its real purpose was to connect the reader with the (deranged) mind of its author rather than to gain acceptance for what was being said. However, as he had done before, he read on and abruptly the tone and the mood of the piece changed.

But then something happened, something was done, something arrived – that dangerous supplement, the principle of division, the devil himself.

With his left hand Finn scooped some Arabica into the cafetiere and poured in the water from the kettle, all the time reading from the papers in his right hand. It appeared as if the 'something' had been caused by the 'appearance' or rather the misperception of the nature of the moon. The author seemed to be saying, incredibly, that up until this point the earth had been flat and it had been perpetual day. Somehow a mistake had been made and the earth had become rounded, meaning that the sun no longer had full dominion, introducing the necessity of night and thence of a nocturnal ruler, a rival to Ra. The apple in the Genesis story was somehow related by a sort of synecdoche to the moon, and the name given to the moon was 'ka', a word translated by Egyptian scholars as 'spirit' but by the author as something closer to 'externalised consciousness', a sort of technology or machine like a written text that appears to have its own life or light, just as the moon does, but actually borrows or steals it. Finn thought of the Ford Ka attempting to run him over the day before and took a break to dispense the coffee, sit down and think.

What was all this shit? An article written by a madman that on any other day would have made absolutely no sense had been granted a sort of relevance and hold over him by a few contiguous details: the car on the poster, the name of his cat and a nutty poem about the moon being a machine. A stubborn rationalist could easily explain away such things, but for Finn there was something in it, something more that he couldn't explain, like a residue that he was unprepared simply to swill away. He pulled the wad of sheets back across the table determined to skim-read the rest, flicked through the articles until he came to one titled 'The Letter K'. More twinges of association. It transpired that what was meant was not so much the letter k as the phoneme /k/, since this could be replaced by the letter c in some words which was presented by the author as a softening or hiding of the letter k (symbolising the true reflection of light by the moon) in the gentler half-moon of the c.

As far as the phoneme /k/ was concerned, the author claimed that it was the enemy of life, that its pronunciation was only possible by temporarily blocking the breath of life (the 'ah' sound) and that, by virtue of when it appeared and what it symbolised, it was an agency in its own right, diasporated across all world languages and invoked like a god whenever it was uttered. The text then listed a thousand or so of the words in English over which it claimed Ka reigned, almost as if the word or the sound gave birth to the thing and not the other way around: /k/atholicism, /k/athedral, /k/ardinal, /k/atechism, /k/anterbury, /k/ancer, /k/arcinogen, /k/ataract, /k/ataclysm, /k/atastrophe, /k/alamity, /k/ash, /k/asino, /k/artel, /k/abal, /k/arnage, /k/arnality, /k/ar, /k/ill, /k/ick, /k/ing/, /k/arma and

/k/atabolism. Given the list, the c argument seemed both cunning and absolutely essential since very few appropriately unpleasant or questionable terms actually began with k, which itself tended to favour oddball connections like kagool, kapok and kangaroo.

He let the coffee rest against his lips without drinking it and enjoyed for a moment the sensation of caffeinated steam drifting up through his nostrils to the apex of his nose and then down the back of his throat. It was three o' clock. He'd been taken in by the thing for more than two hours. Where was the sense of proportion he'd spent so many painful years redeveloping? He had to put all of this into perspective. But what sort of perspective could contain it? Or he had to drop it, ignore it, go into work on Monday and, if the folders were there again, ask some questions, refuse to work on them until he got some kind of sane explanation. But still something nagged at him. Something to do with the letter k. The steam was prickling the hairs in his nose causing a static-like response and – that was it! He blew the coffee half way across the table.

The clicks, the washing together of the sounds and the peculiar clicks. Only they weren't clicks, they were the letter k, or rather, he presumed, the phoneme /k/. Somehow, for some unguessable reason, his mind had been analysing all the speech going on around him and filtering out everything but that one sound. In fact, when he looked back, there was a whole chain of linked events to which the letter k (etc.) was the common key: the advertisement for the Ka, the bird cawing outside the window, K2, Loki, Koresh, the clicks – God, even the 'cacophony' on the radio. His mind banged backwards and forwards between acceptance and denial like a door in a high wind. Open, closed, open, closed – but was open actually open, and was closed really closed? He didn't know, felt really scared now, as if he was falling backwards off a cliff, away from the dull security that he'd built up towards the maelstrom he'd once inhabited and that he thought he'd left well behind. He had to get out, go for a walk, stop himself churning it over. He grabbed his jacket from the hook in the hall and got out of the door before he could think another thought and practically ran all the way down the street, climbing into the first bus he saw when he got to the main road and collapsing into an upstairs seat.

An hour later, having consumed a cappuccino and a chocolate twist at the Caffé Nero on Market Street whilst mindlessly reading tidbits from the local Metro, Finn found himself on the streets again without any clear plan of action. Not the least of his problems was that he couldn't prevent the normally dormant parts of his brain from riffling through their verbal stores for words and phrases containing the letters c and k and then putting them together into arguments and propositions: capitalism and canker, carnage and caduceus, cathedral and cant. It was a catch 22 and he couldn't afford the carriage. It didn't help when he happened to look up on King Street as a beggar asked him for twenty pence only to be greeted by the letters CK emblazoned across a shop window. Calvin Klein! He grinned despite himself and for a moment caught his own reflection in the glass. There was something unhinged about it, and ghostly, as if the contrast was turned up too high.

No, he had to do something to distract himself, something that would hold his attention, tie up his mind. A film perhaps. He started striding towards Oxford Road, walking as briskly as he could without seeming too out of place. Luckily, there was a movie showing he'd been meaning to see again, Ridley Scott's *Alien: The Director's Cut* and he settled down with a coke at the back of the theatre intent on at least an hour and a half's respite. But after the eerie opening, the birth scene, the descent to the planet and the journey to the source of the distress signal, there it was again. John Hurt's character, Kane, infected with an alien parasite, with evil itself. It was impossible for Finn not to think of the parable of Cain and Abel and of the story's pivotal significance as he understood it in Christian theology as the carrying through of the consequences of The Fall and the loss of Eden. Then there was Citizen Kane, the image of whose eponymous hero on a giant screen made him think of Orwell and the phrase 'Big Brother is watching you'. Once again Finn began to experience the very uncomfortable sensation that the world was being screened for his benefit alone, and that he was somehow the butt of its joke, the fall-guy.

The rest of the film passed in a blur of dripping teeth and strobing lights all meshed up with the relentless chatter of the letter k, and it was with some relief that Finn greeted the closing scene of the cat (why a cat?) and Sigourney Weaver finally at peace. Outside it was raining hard and he was forced to shelter under the cinema's canopy until a break in the clouds afforded him the opportunity to make a dash for the bus shelter further down the street. However, as he passed an alley just before the corner of Portland Street, a dark-haired woman dressed in clubbing gear half-concealed by a kagool stepped out from the shadows and time seemed to shudder to a halt, as if her hand had always been meant to reach out to him, as if the proffered flyer had always been intended to find its way into his grasp. He turned it over in stop-frame animation, and took in with aching slowness the fact that it was a VIP invite to the opening of a new club, Club X. He looked up into the woman's face just in time to see her mouth the word:

'Go'

Then she backed out of sight and he was on the move again, time running at twenty-five frames a second, normality resumed.

He'd been afraid it would be something to do with K and the change of letter, of emphasis, of gear even seemed to release him. Why not go along to a club for an hour, have a drink, chill out a little? By sitting in X he would be somehow obscurely outside the dominion of K, inside the walls of another capital city and under its protection. He checked the address. It wasn't far away, just a few streets across the city and he set off with the fervour of a man on the edge of an oasis.

The club itself had once been called Time or Jam or some such thing, he recollected when he arrived at the door, but now the sign was just the single letter, black rimmed with gold, like a hieroglyph in its solitude. As promised, the flyer let him pass unhindered by the expressionless black doormen into the belly of the club which, surprisingly given that it was supposed to be a grand opening, was only about a third full. The crowd was mainly young, dressed in muted tones but with tiny splashes of intense colour here and there and lots of gold, and there was something odd about the atmosphere, a lazy edginess that made Finn think of David Lynch movies he'd seen. At the bar he ordered a red wine spritzer, noticing x's wherever he looked: not only as motif worked through the carpeting and across the girl's T-shirt, but, for heaven's sake, her earrings, even the ice-cubes in the bucket were x-shaped. But still he felt secure as he took a barstool and sipped at the spritzer. After all, an X wasn't a K, was it?

He smoothed down his hair, tried to calm his nerves. All around the club, video screens offered the tantalising image of a near-naked woman sitting in the crutch of a black, x-shaped chair set against a circular inferno of flames, intended presumably to signify desire. On the sound system, mixed in with the low-grade dance beat, Finn fancied he could hear a voice, dark and thick, churned in with the sounds but couldn't make out any words. Boy, but the spritzer tasted good, though, better than anything. But then the lighting changed, the spots down-turned, bathing the club in violet, and as if on cue people started to move tidally across the floor.

It's the violet hour, thought Finn, thinking of Eliot and his faceless office workers trudging mechanically to and from work. At the far end of the club, accompanied by rolling clouds of dry ice and the switching on of a single white spotlight, an enormous man, rhinoceros-like in his hugeness, stepped onto a podium in front of a black, velvet curtain that trembled slightly as if in a gentle breeze.

'Welcome, welcome to the opening of Club X,' he growled, pausing and looking appreciatively around the dimly-lit gathering.

'There is, let us say, a machine,' he continued. 'And behold it knits. It knits us in and it knits us out.'

Finn began to feel queasy, involuntarily gulped for air. There was something not quite right about this. Those surely were not plausible words with which to begin a Grand Opening speech. A wave of nausea swept up through his body, so intense that he retched slightly and the barmaid leant across to ask him whether he was alright, only what she actually seemed to say was:

'You're hollow, a sail with no breeze.'

At the words the snow-shaker of his composure fell and shattered on the floor.

I've been spiked, Finn thought, staring feebly into the empty glass, spiked on the prongs of the K.

In the boiling horror of his mind's eye he saw an imperious X straighten its back and stand up to face a mass rally of the letter A, then his own head swarming with electrodes and on countless screens before him an entire world lock-stepped to the metronomic repetition of a single, senseless word: ka, ka, ka, ka. Somewhere, the fat man was talking about embrocation and celestial oil and it was clear that there was something he wanted to show everyone, something behind a curtain. Spasm after spasm wracked Finn's gut whilst avine talons, a rook or a crow perhaps, raked what was left of his mind, cawing all the while. Through an open window a voice spoke from a velvet sky:

'So it is with great pleasure that I reveal to you the core of our beliefs, the centre of operations, the machine that knits us all, the backer of Club X.'

And with this a cord was pulled and the curtain fell away.

The Long Drive

On the surface, it was a spontaneous gathering, a happening if you like in the Warholian sense. None of the twenty or so individuals crammed around the table and ranged across the floor had planned to be there – they just were. Their presence was apparently, in each case, accidental, purely the product of chance. Somehow, all of their trajectories, regardless of where they'd begun that day or where they'd intended to go, had arrived at the same end – Josh's kitchen. Even Josh hadn't planned to be there, he'd just come back to pick up the wallet he'd forgotten, on his way to the pub. From thereon in it was like an experiment in particle physics where the metronomic chiming of the doorbell invariably marked the introduction of yet another exotic addition to the mix and thereby set in play a whole new combinatorial set of interactions. The eventual result of this, after a dozen or so rings, was that the conversation began to overheat, to boil over and to pass well beyond what seemed to me the acceptable limits of such an event. Indeed, the exchanges became so rapid, the interest so heightened, the laughter and the energy of the contributions so extreme that the air itself seemed to lose its contiguity and in the haze I felt as if I was witnessing the consequences of a sort of breakdown in normal service where the processing was being pushed so fast that the grain, the splicing, the individual frames were becoming evident.

Actually, I only knew three of the people present – Josh, the quizzical host, his housemate Emma with whom I taught Media Studies, and her closest friend Katy. Indeed, my own reasons for being there were as spurious as anyone else's: I'd been having an ill-advised affair with the girlfriend of one of my best friends following their fall-out which, for three months, had been like living out a dream. Unfortunately, that was exactly what it had turned out to be and, a few weeks before, it had come to an abrupt and – in some people's eyes – thoroughly predictable stop. Since then, all other strategies having failed, I had been staking out their house, staring through their windows, raking through their trash, looking for any sort of clue as to where they had gone (I later found out that they'd fled to London before taking teaching jobs in the Middle East). That evening, instead of returning disconsolately home, I'd decided to make a detour in search of company and some way of distracting myself.

Before I knew it, though, I'd unloaded the whole plot, and Josh and the first arrivals reacted to my story of lost love and short-lived joy with incredulity and laughter that hedged somewhere between a superior sort of mockery and downright ridicule.

'How could you be so stupid? That's the most preposterous thing I've ever heard.'

The more I tried to explain the extraordinary things that had happened between us and why I'd decided to take the risk, the more outrageously they laughed and, after a few glasses of wine and a spliff or two, I actually found myself joining in, swept along by the exorbitant jollity that my narrative had seemed to inspire. I guess, looking back, it was as if something gave way inside me and I squandered any love I felt there and then on this one conversation, or as if they were somehow drawing all of the emotion out of me like witch-doctors sucking out the venom from a wound. Perhaps it was precisely this diffusion of what was to me so precious into such an arbitrary assembly that sent up the beacon and started the doorbell ringing. If so, then maybe the relationship wasn't over until that conversation, effectively an act of betrayal, took place. I didn't know. I didn't want to know. Whatever the case, within a couple of hours a party, almost a celebration, was in full swing around me: jubilant faces, red wine sloshing in mugs, insistent techno simmering on the hi-fi, people peroxiding their hair – it was as if in spilling out my guts I'd somehow provided the impetus for a whole, new, revolutionary movement.

I told only one more story that night. Someone, I think his name was Ed, had brought the subject around to that of the police, and his account of meeting a plain-clothes officer at Glastonbury who knew more about him than he should have done reminded me of a dream an ex-girlfriend of mine had once told me. In the dream, I was an artist and we were living in a garret room. I was painting a large canvas in the middle of the studio when there was a knock at the door and the police burst in. They examined the room from end to end, looking in every conceivable place for whatever it was they were after, searching space itself. Whilst they searched, becoming more and more exasperated as their probing revealed nothing of any consequence, my girlfriend noticed that the painting I was working on was composed not of splashes of colour and finely sketched lines as she had supposed but writing, minute handwriting, swathes of it, and as she watched she realised that this was what the police were after but were unable to see. This was my crime – I was a writer, not a painter but the police were too stupid, too trapped within the barracks of their methodology, to see through the subterfuge.

When I had finished, Josh leant back in his chair, fixed me with a subjugating gaze and commented with a slight smirk: 'They said that my theories had nothing to do with science but instead were more a matter for the police.'

Apparently it was something that Freud had once said about his detractors.

Quite late on, it must have been after twelve, and feeling simultaneously elated at having unburdened myself (the rapid release of energy being correlated with pleasure) and yet somehow obscurely depressed, I waved goodbye to everyone and made my exit. It was a night in early February and, in contrast with the molten temperatures indoors, frost coated the path and the unkempt bush to the left of the gate and the frozen air tortured my lungs. My car was parked across the other side of the cul-de-sac and as I approached it I noticed something odd about the passenger door. Looking at it from an angle so that the streetlight refracted off the thin, sparkling layer of frost, I initially saw only a series of slashes that I took for a random act of vandalism. On looking more closely, however, I saw that they had been made by a fingernail without damaging the paintwork and that the three lines joined together to form the letter K. Standing there in the cold and the moonlight, suddenly very alone, the letter K seemed like a very intimidating thing for someone to have scrawled on my car. Not initials or a slogan, which would have been understandable, but a frost-etched glyph that in its isolation and manner of inscription was somehow more chilling and symbolic than it should have been.

I smoothed it out of existence with a quick stroke of my hand, not wanting to feel marked as I drove home, and set about clearing the windscreen and the other windows with a scraper. It had been a strange evening, one in which I'd inadvertently opened up my heart and experienced the exhilaration of a very large expenditure. But consequently I now felt very much the poorer, like a failed gambler outside a casino. Also, there had been something faintly sinister about the way the conversation had kept veering onto the topic of the police, almost a logic of implication leading from confession to punishment. I wondered if, in some sense, my affair had actually been criminal, a fake, a forgery, something that had not been evident until I had revealed my thoughts and motivation just now. In other words, a matter for the authorities. What was worse – I wondered whether I had actually told the truth or just blurted something out for the sake of filling the air, shooting the breeze.

Climbing into the car, I felt the head-set of paranoia descend and fit into place, gripping my cranium tightly in its jaws. Rather than an impromptu party, the gathering at Josh's house now felt like it had been a court staffed by highly-skilled interlocutors who, working as a team, had cleverly hustled the truth out of me. Even as I sat there, their verdict was going out across the wire and finely-tuned instincts were beginning to twitch. Maybe that was precisely how the police were selected, on the basis of what hadn't been educated out of them, their gut-feeling. I was going to be picked up, I knew I was. Picked up and interrogated for crimes against love, treachery of the worst kind. For the truth was that, somehow, that evening, I had given up even the ghost of the fight against inevitability and allowed myself to be sucked into a cheap, discursive act of betrayal. Suddenly, I was drenched with sweat and filled with a dread that was wholly out of proportion to the situation. The dope together with the peculiar trends in the conversation, seemed to have sensitised me to a completely different dimension of experience and I felt as if I was experiencing reality on two levels at the same time: that of the everyday and of ordinary consciousness but also something much deeper and more connected, almost a symbolic commentary on what was actually at stake.

I snapped my favourite tape into the player to try and bring myself back to earth and stop the churning in my head. The familiar liquid sounds and rounded bass of Dreadzone filled the car and allowed my reasoning with myself to bite. The worst that could happen was that I would be pulled over for driving erratically or for being slightly pissed. As far as I knew, they didn't have a test for measuring how stoned you were. That said, I could still sense the other part of my mind telling me that this wasn't the point, not the point at all. The problem was that I would respond to being stopped on the unconscious level, having been finally caught out, and break down, screaming:

'Yes, you're right. Arrest me. I am that man, the one you've been looking for. The devil himself. For so long now I've been hiding in the light, but no more, no more. Take me away.'

I started up the car and rolled slowly forwards. The journey was only about twenty miles, fifteen through towns and then five along country back-roads, but I knew I was going to experience every inch of it as an ordeal. In fact, even now, as I pulled out onto the A6 and started on the long drive that would take me to and then around the city centre before spitting me out onto Oldham Road, I realised that I was covering the tarmac at a rate somewhat less than fifteen miles an hour. I had to speed up, had to blend in with the other drivers and not draw attention to myself. I pressed down on the accelerator and watched the needle climb up to thirty. So far, so good. The deserted streets of Longsight, never friendly even during the day, scrolled past my window like pages on a microfiche but slowly, agonisingly slowly. And all the time my eyes flicked back and forth between the road, the rear-view and the side mirrors, looking for the slightest hint of blue or white. I pulled a cigarette out of the pack on the passenger seat and lit it cagily, swerving slightly as I did so. By the time I reached the roundabout at the foot of the Mancunian Way the music had segued into Autechre's disconcerting 'Flutter', and I realised somehow from the discomfort of the beats, that I was completely hunched up over the steering wheel and barely breathing. From the outside it must have looked as if the car was being driven by a raven or a crow. I pushed myself back in the seat, straightened my body up, bracing my arms against the spokes of the wheel and breathed in deeply.

It was going okay. I was a third of the way in, and all I had to do to keep on treading the line, obey all the signs and restrictions and I was home and dry. I was also trying to keep my mind clear of any thoughts or suggestions regarding the police and the possibility of my being stopped. This was built upon the superstitious premise that perhaps I was creating my own reality and that by thinking something, I made it all the more likely that it would happen. However, as is often the case, the more I tried to exclude this possibility from my thoughts, the more it vied for my attention. I eventually realised that the only way to keep it at bay was to fill my mind with the material trivia of the journey: the shops, the road-signs, the odd pedestrian, the litter on the road. Ironically, it was just as I switched to this alternative tack that a dark-blue car cruised up behind me and took up the sort of measured distance and tracking position that told me immediately I was under surveillance.

I don't know how I managed to stay on the road. Perhaps it was simply that the shock, despite all my foreboding, caused my arms to lock and thereby kept me on course. Part of me wanted to stop, there and then, and get it over with, fall down sobbing in the road, but the older, deeper instinct to get away with it kicked in, flicking my body onto automatic and forcing me entirely out of myself. For the next four or five miles I found myself driving like an automaton, demonstrating how perfectly I could turn with the road, brake at traffic signals, use my indicators and keep on the right side of the road. Throughout the whole of that distance the dark-blue car maintained its relative position precisely and I felt as if all of my observable behaviour was being tested, measured against some fixed standard of normality. It was almost as if the shadowy figures behind were already inside the car, probing its innards, searching for any flaw in my integrity that would trip the hair-trigger of their suspicion.

But my performance must have been faultless because, shortly after entering Oldham, they indicated right and peeled off, leaving me with a clear run ahead largely along country lanes. I breathed out very loudly and banged hard on the steering wheel with both hands. It had happened just as I had expected, but I had passed the test. There was to be no humiliating collapse in the face of authority, no snivelling wretchedness as my true crimes were read out. I felt released as if from a jail sentence, on the outside again, back in manual and, in want of some way of celebrating the fact, I pressed down harder on the accelerator and made the car speed up the hill out towards open country and freedom. Within minutes I was doing fifty, sixty, seventy, coursing through the sleepy hamlets on the tops like a river in full flood, slaloming round the bends, filled once more with the joy of the earlier part of the evening, of being inside in the warmth of society rather than out in the cold. It was thus in a state of wreckless abandon that I skied past the crossroads two miles or so from my house and failed to notice the snout of a patrol car protruding from the side road. But as I plunged down the next hill, it wasn't possible to miss the blue light that stole into the car and fluttered around like a trapped bird.

Fuck. Now I was for it. There was no chance now of playing safe. Instead there was a stark choice: stop and face up, or run for it. Without slowing down, I quickly calculated the relationship between the distance still to go and the start I had on the police car, which was considerable. I could do it, I thought, I could outrun them. On any other day, I would have stopped and taken the rap, but that night, because of the dope, the turn of the conversation and my resultant paranoia, I simply couldn't afford to do it. I was too much in the other realm and, like the guiltiest of children facing the most authoritarian of fathers, I could not be found out. So I put my foot down, floored the accelerator and the short race home, the perfect complement to the long, painstaking drive, began. Within seconds I was at the turning to Delph and managing not to oversteer as I slewed around the corner and pelted up the short stretch to the centre of the village. As I reached the sharp right-angle between the houses that would've taken me to my street, and at which I would have to brake hard, I glanced in the mirror and saw that they had just made the previous turning and were throttling up, intent on giving full chase.

With a sharp left jerk on the wheel I made the car slide sideways into Stoneswood Road and started up the hill, but then thought that it would be much cleverer not to park outside my house but instead to pull into the short lane on the right and walk away from the car. Without really thinking about what I was doing, I switched my headlights off and turned into the lane, screaming up it to the top before, in one, rapid movement, pulling on the handbrake, taking out the ignition key and stepping out of the car. Instantly, the car, having been a living beast of fire and fury, was reduced to a dead thing, something I could walk away from easily, something I could disown as if it had been the car that had been at fault, not me. As I walked, the police car nosed into the bottom of the lane, stopped and two men got out. I continued strolling down, completely carried away with myself, unable to think or feel or do anything but maintain the lie, and as I moved towards them, so they moved towards me, the distance closing very fast until it was the moment of truth. I knew they hadn't actually seen me get out of the car so I did have a chance, but there again I was the only other person on the lane so it didn't require a genius to work out who the likely culprit was. Speed and direction were all. By coming at them rather than running away, I was confounding their expectations, in addition to which, by allowing there to be no let up in the pace of events, I was challenging them to think at the most rapid rate possible, at the rate that reality itself was unfolding. Without consciousness in other words.

As we met, I could see that their eyes were fixed more on the car than on me and all it took was a brief 'Evening' and I was past them and gone. One of them looked across at me and I picked up a slight flicker of hesitation but it was not enough to make him check, not enough to enable him to break in on the confidence and purposefulness of my stride. I seemed to know what I was doing there and where I was going whereas they did not, and perhaps it was this slight edge that proved to be the deciding factor. However, once I'd rounded the corner and had a little time in which to think I didn't feel anything like so self-assured. It would only take them a few more seconds to realise that I was in all probability the driver, and that didn't give me enough time to get all the way up the hill and in through my front door. I could run, but then they would know for sure that it was me, and anyway, I felt too physically drained almost to move at all. No, I would have to hide somewhere and wait for them to go. I looked around the road and saw that there was a large bush to the right of the nearest house, a scraggy sort of thing to be sure, but enough to conceal me on what was, due to the cloud cover, now a very dark night. So I slipped myself in behind it, squatted down and waited.

For ten minutes or so I heard nothing. No voices, no footsteps, no car starting. Frost, melted by my breathing, dripped down onto my face and I could feel my hair striating as the water began to run in occasional rivulets down my forehead and off my nose. I shifted position and tried to remember whether I'd changed my address to the new house on my license or on the car's vehicle registration form. I was pretty sure I hadn't, it wasn't the sort of thing I ever did – another example of my petty lawlessness. Then I heard the scrunch of gravel and a low murmuring that sounded like it was coming from just around the corner of the house next to me. Instinctively, I sank backwards and tried to shrink myself as near as I could to nothingness. It was them, I was sure of it, and they were trying to figure out where I had gone. Sitting there behind the bush, catching ever so often the vague scent of rosemary or was it lavender, it occurred to me that there was something intensely familiar about the situation. Not just that I had been there, or somewhere like, it many times before, but that things had always been like this, that the entire day was like the story of my life spelt out in a single, extraordinary sentence. Everything followed from the frustration of the original impulse – and there was always someone standing in the driveway, always a father of some kind, a figure of authority, a policeman.

I thought they were going to find me. At that moment, I truly believed they were more than just policemen but agents of a higher authority and that the crime I had committed was the most heinous in the book. But they didn't. The harsh chatter on their walkie-talkies led them nowhere and, after a few minutes, their voices drifted off and I heard the slam of doors and an engine starting. I had got away with it. I was safe, in the clear.

Back finally in the warmth and comfort of the house, though, things didn't seem so straightforward. It had been a long drive, the drive of my life but where exactly had I arrived at the end of it? I was alone, I was drained, the radio in the sitting room had the look to me of a listening device and the way the shadows moved across the wall made me think over and again that there was someone else in the room, someone who very definitely wasn't me. I switched on the television to try and fill the void and, as it hummed briefly before starting up, I half-imagined for a moment that the image when it finally appeared would be of a face, frozen, caught in the headlights. Underneath there would be a number to call if you had any information, and nonsensically the number would be mine.

Sweet Peas

You were at the end of the line, you knew that. At the terminus. Fucked and humiliated beyond belief. You had vowed that if you ever ended up back at your mother's, your life having turned to mush once again, you would commit suicide. Yet here you were, standing in the kitchen and talking as if nothing had really happened, as if Krakatoa hadn't blown up for the second time in your face, as if the world could simply carry on spinning listlessly through the void without evincing the slightest sign of being affected by your plight. You were broke, you were homeless, you hadn't worked properly for over a year, and the worst of it was that it had all happened, just the same way, once before. Then you had been running scared from a bunch of criminals who'd shaved your head, stolen your money and deposited you in a derelict mental hospital which they'd given you to understand they were going to burn down with you in it. Then you'd been terrified even of your own shadow cast against the decaying walls by the single candle they'd left you to keep out the darkness. This time the details were different, no doubt about that. But the underlying pattern was the same. You had got involved with something deeper, darker and more powerful than yourself. All of your friendships, all of the ties that secured you to your previous life had been severed, reduced to shreds. You had had to run, to seek sanctuary in order to save your soul, and here she was, your mother, repeating the same phrase she'd used then, the exact same words in the same season:

'Well, I suppose you could take down the sweet peas.'

Two breakdowns in normal service, one compounded upon the other. It was too much to bear, too much like extreme carelessness. As a child, you had to struggle to keep your head above water, had to fight to stop yourself succumbing to the lethal dullness of it all. For weeks at a time, you had stopped speaking, or behaved with the mechanical mien of a broken robot, experimented with your demeanour to see if it made any difference, but if anything was ever noticed it was not commented upon, and the pantechnicon of parental indifference had rolled on regardless. Ten years ago, your father had died of a massive heart attack whilst pulling up cemented fence posts, like a latter-day Moses bringing his commandments up the mountain to God, and from that time forwards, from the moment you saw death inscribed across the parchment of his face, you had been a fugitive, escaping one unbearable situation only to find yourself becoming rapidly immersed in another. Like a bad penny rolling down a cratered high street, you'd spun and temporarily shone before disappearing from view, popping up again here and there only to be cast down, as if your fleeting appearances were all the excuse that was needed for the mechanics of your destitution to whirr back into action. And here you were, in another gully, another pock-mark, deeper and more dangerous than the rest because more advanced, and the conversation was about flowers.

You say of course you'll do it, anything to help, but the phraseology, the precise mimicking of word and tone cause you to falter slightly as you reply. My time is over, you think, my passage through the light, and all you can talk about is dismantling some plants, but you say nothing, bend under, maintain the façade. As you pass through from the kitchen into the conservatory, you see that, despite it being late August, the sun is bearing down upon the world from a clear sky like an irate priest, spreading its gospel of orange and yellow, burning into the rockery and lasering the bird table. You pause to collect the secateurs before moving out into the garden, the words still thrumming, on the stretched canvas of your mind. What is it about this time of year, you wonder, that makes it so apposite, and why the sweet peas? Why not the carrots or the cabbages, the honeysuckle or the clematis? You walk in a daze past the faded yellow of the verbascum, the hooded red and blue of the salvia and the dark wine of the scabious, noticing nothing, your mind researching connotations. You remember a poem you wrote years before called 'Give Peas A Chance', which concerned the weekly battles you and your sister waged with your parents over the eating of green vegetables. In the poem, whilst it was peas that were the pawns in an on-going war of attrition, almost a siege like the one that befell Mont Segur in Southern France during the persecution of the Cathars, it turned out that the real peas, the peas that counted, were the off-spring, the siblings, the children who vomited their way through a never-ending succession of Sundays and were crushed beneath the yoke of blind insistence. So perhaps the sweet peas were symbolic, coded references leading to a subterranean cavern of concealed meanings? You pause by the purple trusses of phlox and gaze into the pond, your eyes chasing the movements of the fish as they twist and turn, scintillating the sunlight.

Certainly, things can mean more than they appear to do on the surface. Four years earlier, just before the denouement which found you washed up and abandoned in the hospital, a girl had handed you a book called 'The Transparency of Evil' and its theme had proved uncannily prescient. Nature runs deep and its interlacing roots make many unseen connections. You finger the secateurs, opening them up and testing their sharpness with your thumb. What to make of it all? You set off towards the bottom garden, through the gate and along the hedged corridor, barely noticing the white of the astrantia, the intense yellow of the coreopsis, trampling the grass and leaves carelessly underfoot as your thoughts grope ahead towards the trellises. Why do I have to think like this, you wonder? Why do I appear to be under such an obligation? Is it because, at the heart of things, there was always an emptiness, a vacuum, an unspoken core that had to be avoided at all costs and into which nobody dared venture?

You reach the black, iron gate and lift the squealing latch, brushing aside the golden rod and the sun-like rudbeckia as you pass. Before you, the lawn stretches out towards the fruit trees and from there past the compost heaps down to the stream. To the left, tethered to a dozen or so canes, stand the Sweet Peas, winnowed slightly from their supports by the gentle, afternoon breeze. Looking at them now, brought stiffly to attention though resisting the call with a few dozen multicoloured flowers, you are reminded obscurely of your father, a man of upright moral and physical bearing, but also of your mother. Indeed, the ensemble seems to you to state a dialectic in horticultural form between enforced rectitude of a sort on the one side and chaotic, natural growth on the other, and as you approach them, you find yourself scrutinising their precise construction as never before. Running between the canes are four lines of twine that keep them a measured distance apart, and the individual plants are tied at intervals seven or eight times to ensure that they keep growing upwards and towards the sun. Now, at the end of their life though there are still many pastel-shaded flowers left on each stem, they tower above you like a strange, floral chequer-board, a monument to a summer of pain-staking diligence.

Feeling the sun boring into your back, you take off your jumper and prepare to engage the enemy, starting off by snipping, one by one, the green ties that affix the stalks to the bamboo, working your way up. As you labour, your mind chisels away at the more abstruse aspects of the task in hand, unwilling to take it lying down. The canes immediately make you think of discipline and punishment. True, you were

never caned at school or by your father, but you felt the flat
of his hand many times and he was somebody who believed
in enforced righteousness rather than the sort of learning
that is acquired by trial and error. To err, in his book, was not
to be human, even as a child, but to be in need of correction,
and you could see – quite blatantly, in fact – that the canes
had something of the same logic about their function. On
top of this, there was the issue of why the plants needed any
interference or guidance at all. You find yourself wondering
what a sweet pea would look like in the wild, and conclude
that, not being a natural climber, they would wind round and
round on themselves and form a sort of bush. What was the
problem with this? It must have something to do with the
flowers, you think, and in particular with the straightness of
their stems. Training them using the canes made them grow
in such a way that they could be stood up easily in vases and
put on display.

There is so much contained in that single train of thought
that you are forced to stop and take a few seconds out to
ponder it. Is this the unconscious logic encased within the
superficially innocent request? Is this the truth of the matter,
and is the point that you be brought up face-to-face with it,
forced to engage manually with the conditions of your own
subjection? It seems so manifest, so crystal clear, that you feel
for a moment like a child staring into the embers of a fire and
seeing monstrous shapes, whole worlds evolve and die in a
moment. Is it real? Can it be trusted? And, if so, what then?
Where does it lead? You take a turn around the orchard to
escape the nettling of the questions and are momentarily
startled when a large cooking apple falls to the ground
behind you with a sickening thud. When you return to the
job you do so with renewed vigour, gripping the delicate
plants firmly, removing the flowers with care but then
uprooting the stalks with unbridled savagery whilst
wrenching up the canes and casting them down with utter
disdain. All the time, though, there is an admixture of

emotions building up inside you, a confused well that, although seeking expression, knows no simple form or language. You bite back tears, but also find yourself laughing, curse aloud angrily but then catch yourself chuckling at the ludicrousness of it all. 'Me and my sister, the sweet peas!' you call out to the pink and white blooms of echinacea and the cobalt petals of the michaelmas daisies. 'Annuals rather than perennials!' you joke to a squirrel, or to the trees, or to nobody in particular.

An hour later and it is all done. The trusses have been removed, the plants dismantled, the sticks taken down and the salvageable flowers arranged in bunches on the grass. You take the straggling remains and cast them onto the mound of twigs, leaves and assorted garden rubbish at the edge of the lawn before setting it on fire. Then you bind together the canes with the left-over twine and carry them down to the garden shed. You have a little trouble again with the padlock, old and rusty as it is, and the hinges scream as you pull back the door but eventually you are inside. Moving quietly in the darkness, anxious not to disturb the myriad of objects balanced precariously on the shelves and cause an avalanche, you find the place and, gently, respectfully, almost reverentially, you lay the bundle of canes down in the space between the rakes and hoes on the one hand, and the shadowy, barely discernible, almost negligible form of the body on the other. 'Only kidding,' you mutter and turn to go, but you never leave. Perhaps you walk head-first straight into a protruding nail, skewering yourself upon your own callousness. Or the author, having alienated himself even from the paper upon which he writes, gives up the ghost and lays his pen aside, leaving you freeze-framed in the doorway. But what is certain is that you remain in the shed for all eternity, trapped in a tableaux from which there is no simple escape.

Shopping List

H was something of a terrorist. Of course, not the sort that hijacks planes or blows things up or exposes random tranches of the civilian population to poisonous gases. No, he was too much of a one-man outfit for all of that. In fact, strictly speaking, he didn't so much spread terror as disseminate disquiet, but he was serious about what he did, deadly serious, and he'd been conducting his unsettling crusade for almost three years now.

It had all started way back when he had been a bored and disillusioned lecturer in a further education college, teaching computer studies to the fickle youth of a northern town. Blair had just come into power – or B liar as he preferred now to call him – and, ever so subtly, minute degree by minute degree, something had happened to the entire machinery of education, a sea change comparable not to the shift from steam power to oil but rather to that which saw the telephone replace the telegraph, a gradualism that was almost an alteration only in the lettering. He'd struggled on for another couple of years, sensing the switch-over but unable to get to grips with it, becoming progressively more alienated from his colleagues, more out of touch with his students, until one day the roof had caved in on his particular model of the world.

He'd gone out late-night to buy something to eat, and found himself traipsing the cavernous aisles of a large convenience store without a shopping list. He didn't have the slightest clue what he wanted, and previously this characteristic lack of foresight hadn't proved too much of a problem, but this time things were different. This time, as he tried to take in the multitude of choices, the panoply of options and variations, he felt himself getting further and further away from making a selection and becoming increasingly more agonised by the paralysing array of goods on offer until, after half an hour or so, he came to a complete halt in front of the soft drinks section. 'I have to get out of here,' he had thought, 'or else I'm going to go totally nuts,' and he had run full tilt out of the store, not caring whether the security guards tried to stop him, not bothering about anything other than arriving at a region beyond choosing, a place where you didn't have to state your being in terms of brands and promotions, offers and deals.

A week later he had given up the fight, whatever it was, and resigned his job, to the transparent joy of many in the establishment. He had become so unable to plan ahead that he froze every morning within minutes of waking up like a crashed computer, and so completely incapable of making a decision between this or that alternative, the one hand or the other, that it was all he could do to make his own breakfast. Then there was the six months in which he did nothing at all, saw no one and descended into a listless sort of hell, like a machine deprived of its instructions, followed by the attempt at suicide when the money ran out and the two and a half months in a psychiatric hospital. It was there, though, in the warm, sheltered, uterine environment of the ward, that he had worked out bit by bit what had actually occurred.

It was the fall of the Berlin Wall that had started it, an event that he had felt happening inside his own mind, as if left and right, conscious and unconscious, were no longer properly separable upon any condition, as if tyranny were exchanged for freedom, freedom for tyranny in a way that converted each into the same thing: one megalithic ideology no longer capable of being checked, or stopped or even made apparent. Thus – or so his thinking ran – did a newly rejuvenated form of capitalism pour through the breaches in the Wall, thus did the cars drive from West to East, trailing consumerism and commodification in their wake, thus did the old world die to make way for the new. From there the thoughts led in a kind of a flurry to the understanding that what had happened with Blair and with the college was not just the unopposable application of the laws of the market and the consequent loss of any genuinely socialist parties, but the conversion of human beings and their society from the analogue to the digital system, and of the flow of love into the bitstream of cold, individualistic calculation. As a computing lecturer he should have seen this much earlier, should have realised that he was part of the problem. Now, it was easy, so easy to see that nothing was real any more but rather just a version of what it used to be, that all that was left were products and goods, discrete units separated from their origins and repackaged for a market so saturated in advertising and the language of consumption that it could no longer think straight. Where people had once possessed traits and characteristics, they were increasingly only thinkable in terms of ingredients and formulae, brands and slogans, and where someone's presence had once been their most significant attribute, it was everyday more the case that it was their absence that counted, their lack of being, as they circled the daily cyclotron of existence like particles of anti-matter, unable to touch upon any condition. Nobody dreamt this would become the case, that negative forms of communication that contained no actual contact with the source like texting and emailing, would promote such a wholesale transformation. But it was, in H's view, undoubtedly so, and it was from this vantage-point that he discovered his vocation, and it was in this facility, this ease of viewing, that he found his true purpose. Henceforth, he would fuck up the process whereby things were bought and sold and profits made, he would have a shopping list and on it would be the multifarious ways in which an individual, operating solo, could interfere and mess with the machines and systems of mercantile exchange.

To begin with, all of his actions had been fairly petty. For instance, he would enter a shop and try on every jumper in a particular range, as if he had no concept of his own size, or, attempting to buy shoes, he would repeatedly place them on the wrong feet as if not understanding the distinction between right and left. Other days, he would work out a hit-list and then engage salesperson after salesperson in protracted and pointless discussions about the precise specifications of items, progressively narrowing down his interest question by question until it became so microscopic that they had to hold up their hands in frank despair. He would also shift price tags around or relocate promotions such that they seemed to imply that televisions were going for as little as thirty-five pence, or that – OFFER MUST END TUESDAY! – onions cost a hundred pounds each, and only a hundred and fifty if you bought two. More recently, he had taken to inserting anti-consumerist slogans into the pockets of trousers and coats or sticking them on cartons and packages, such as 'Buy Less, Live More,' 'The Price is Wrong', 'Labour Made Me' or 'Contains Wasps' and for entertainment at the end of a hard day, he would fill a trolley with a mountain of goods, run them through the checkout only to claim, in all sincerity, that he had forgotten his wallet and walk out of the store.

He knew that most of his campaigns were not particularly well-aimed and that, more often than not, it was the lowly sales staff or the customers who had to pick up the pieces after him, but equally he was aware that he had no real way of reaching the true culprits even if they weren't victims themselves, and that, short of melting down every coin and burning every note, there was no better way for him to carry out his attacks than to mount a solitary jihad against the churches and cathedrals, the chapels and basilicas of capital that at least gave him the satisfaction of knowing that he was doing something, that he wasn't taking the whole thing lying down. All the same, secrecy being essential in his line of work, it was a lonely sort of occupation, and thus he interspersed it with periods of regular employment, working casually for the very stores that he most despised, periods that would begin well but slowly descend into chaos and farce as he started to give things away or charge ridiculous prices or insist that the customer trade in themselves in part exchange for the merchandise.

This latter stunt had given him the idea for the action in which he was involved today, the most elaborate and carefully-worked out of all his plays, and one which was the culmination of over six months planning and subterfuge. He would put himself on the market, and then try to buy himself. In order to make this happen, he had taken a job with a nearby supermarket and slowly worked his way up from the sales-tills to the management office, trading on the fact that he could type and that he was 'somebody who's good with computers'. Indeed, the computer, the main-frame that ran the whole of the store's operations, was his target and it was remarkable that he – an urban guerrilla and somebody about whom his managers knew practically nothing – found himself within four months inside the holy of holies and inserting a new product onto the stocklist together with a mini-program which, when triggered, would cause all hell to break lose.

In support of the central thrust of his operation, he had been conducting research into various ways of tracing barcodes onto different parts of his body such that they could be picked up by shop scanners. He had begun by drawing them with permanent ink onto the palm of his hand and flashing them through the red laser light when nobody was watching, but although this method had worked once and he had seen the magical words 'Baked Beans – 35p' come up on the display, it was by no means reliable and thus he had abandoned it. Eventually, after several false starts and having considered even tattooing, he had found a T-shirt printer who knew a lot about transfers and who could generate a copy on acetate that would print perfectly onto his skin with the mere application of warm water. This, slightly enlarged and embellished onto the flattest part of the back of his hand, had worked every time that he had tried it, and it was thus, suitably adorned, on this, the day of days, that H found himself four back in the queue at his local branch of Asda, waiting after work with his trolley-load for the true accounting to begin.

Nobody spoke to each other. Nobody ever seemed to speak when they were in the line-up, almost as if what lay ahead of them was a police photographer or a firing squad rather than a place where they could show off their bank card or make a great fuss over affixing their personalised signature to the contractual receipt. The woman in front of him, H couldn't help noticing, seemed to live off a diet entirely composed of biscuits, crisps and chocolate milk. He choked back a number of uncomplimentary thoughts whilst shifting nervously from foot to foot, swaying forwards to let a man with pasty, dough-like skin pass behind him holding his meagre basket like a mascot high in the air. Glancing upwards, he gazed into the gratuitous maw of the vacant space above that seemed such an essential accompaniment to the shopping experience. 'Like the vaults of the Vatican,' he thought to himself, shuffling slightly forwards as he sensed that the queue had moved on.

Finally, it was his turn and he began to unload all of the randomly selected goods onto the moving conveyor. One by one, the young man at the till swiped them mindlessly through the shimmering, interlaced lines, pausing only to repeat the pass when an item failed to trigger the obligatory beep. Tuna, peppercorns, sanitary towels, dog food. As he worked, H stood by the chute and assembled the packets and cartons into the bags without looking, attending only to the second-to-last item and thereby the moment just before the Total button would be hit. It was a four-pack of toilet rolls and, as it arrived in front of him and the operator turned back to the belt, he slipped the back of his right hand surreptitiously over the scanner, held it there and waited. It must have been only a second before it registered, but for that second H felt as if he had plunged under water and entered the deep where only bloated and protuberant creatures slowly grazed far from the light. Then it happened.

Later that night, alone and back at his flat, H reflected on the purity, the pristine beauty of his action. The words 'Human Being' and the price '£17.56' (the cost, as calculated by him, of the body's constituent chemicals) appearing on the item display screen not only at his till but at all of the others simultaneously. The fact that they had remained there for a good minute or so in order that their import could be properly taken on board whilst the employees scrabbled at their keyboards and attempted to ring for assistance, following which the screens had blurred and the till printers sprung back into action as they attempted to process a download of every single product in the store. From then on chaos began to break out here and there, slowly at first, but quickly gathering pace like fire in gorse; people abandoning their trolleys, others simply packing up what they could grab hold of and walking out of the store, managers running backwards and forwards trying to stop the relentless chatter of the machines, a voice over the intercom requesting co-operation but finding itself unable to break through the din of voices. Meanwhile, after dousing himself in the scene for a few minutes, H had quietly leant over, ripped the spiralling receipt from its holder and walked out of the store, revealing the barcode emblazoned across his T-shirt as he did so together with the slogan 'Are You On The List?'

Looking about the room now though, and feeling the emptiness cramp around him like an ill-fitting jacket, he wondered about it all. Wasn't it true that he had become precisely that which he so hated, a digitised unit bereft of the ties and affiliations to the sine wave of friendship and affection that marked out the human from the mechanical, the subject from the object? A vacant lot? A mere parking space of a person? Certainly, his surroundings did not speak of love or warmth or social success. It was always a shame that he couldn't share his achievements with anyone, but this was not only because of the attendant risks but also, much more importantly, because there was nobody left to tell them to. He had disappeared completely, that was the truth of it, dropped out of social reality like a stone, and, although it had been necessary in order to accomplish his mission, it was an excruciatingly lonely way to mark out your existence. Besides which, whatever he did, it didn't really make much more than a scintilla of difference in the grand scheme of things, although perhaps if he persevered then he, and others like him, would prove to be the glass in the road that tripped up the juggernaut. That said, taken in the context of the others, it had been a good day, and tomorrow would be better. Tomorrow would be much better. Tomorrow, somehow, he would re-brand the sky.

Transparency

The Myth of the Self
    Years ago, yes, it is certain, I existed. I was there and nobody could have convinced me otherwise. I lived, I breathed, I loved, I listened and I was. Then, somehow, one day, this ceased to be the case. I became simply a word in a sentence, a meme in an escalatory narrative, a vagrant in semiotic hell. As a result, the world converted wholesale into a series of differential impressions refracted through the distorting lens of a mythical self in which I was compelled to believe or lose everything. Henceforth, I was to be a storyteller, a spinner of webs, a weaver of fictions, not just when I chose to be but all of the time, every day, world without end, amen. And the self in whom I was forced to place my faith and in whose ghostly wake I now struggled to read my immanence went from that moment onto a kind of life-support that, although negligible at first, gradually took over, overwhelming its host and reducing him by stages to the inscrutable status of a cipher, a punctuation mark, and finally, the white space of the page itself.

Maiden looked sidelong at the steam rising spasmodically from the mug of chicken soup on the table's edge and sighed. It was not going well. There was to be no salvation in fiction, at least not today. The sixth and last story, the one that was supposed to pull all of the others together, and it read more like a philosophical treatise than a compulsive narrative. More like a granite wall than a gently curving forest path. He stood up and stretched his arms, ran a hand through his tangled mess of hair and looked around the strangely comforting horror that was his flat. All of the furniture was

99

fourth, fifth, sixth or seventh-hand – frayed, ragged and covered, like the tattered carpet, with cigarette burns and stains whose history Maiden could have recollected had anyone been available to ask him. The walls were spattered with what looked like blood but was actually a painterly mixture of cayenne pepper and tomato juice, the final exposition of an evening of particular self-loathing that had taken place some months ago. Jars, plates, crushed cider cans and empty food packaging littered the floor, each receptacle filled with its own unique cache of cigarette butts and the paraphernalia of joint production.

Pinned to the walls and even to some of the furniture were photographs, torn newspaper articles and club flyers, shards left over from a period when his life had had a more external dimension to it, and behind the sofa were stuffed thousands of pages of late night musings, endless moments of clarity which he'd been forced to write down or lose, hoping one day to turn them into something coherent. Picking its way gingerly through the rubble, seemingly oblivious to the arcane significance of all of the objects, Maiden's cat Deus stopped and looked up at him, momentarily awed perhaps that something in the flat other than itself seemed to contain life. It miaowed briefly and then returned to its daily task of patrolling what remained of the floor space and looking for stray threads dangling from the furniture or rolled up balls of paper to alleviate the monotony.

'The cat that I see and the cat that is seen are not the same,' thought Maiden. 'One is the myth of the other, and neither is real.' The thought provided him with little comfort, seemed in fact to crystallise his current difficulties with the story. He realised that he was losing touch with common-sense, everyday reality, largely as a consequence of having withdrawn or having been allowed to withdraw so totally from it. He hadn't left the flat for three weeks having decided to seal himself off for the writing of the six stories, and for that whole time he had been living off packet soup, pasta and tins of one sort and another. His telephone was cut off, the television showed only the number three superimposed upon fuzz on all channels and there had not been a single visitor. But far from feeling down about it, he felt almost proud of his achievement, as if he had refined isolation to a high art and, in celebration, he had a few days earlier pulled the thick curtains shut in every room and closed out the sunlight for good until it was over. The last human sound he'd heard had been a voice on the phone before it was disconnected and even that was a wrong number, a Tim somebody or other trying to get hold of a long-lost friend. Maiden had read about people dying in their homes and not being found for months, even years in some cases, and whilst the world had expressed its outrage at the fact that such a thing could happen in a civilised society, he had been almost impressed. 'How to disappear completely', he had thought, and had even planned at one point to write a handbook on the subject, on how you could gradually become so transparent, so diaphanous, that people literally looked right through you, ignored your presence, forgot that you existed. Because, of course, the self is and is only ever a myth of self, a fiction which we sell to both ourselves and others, and it is sustained only on the condition that we sustain it in others, socially collaborate in the essential fakery of it all. Or so Maiden thought, remembering the moment at his father's funeral when, standing by the graveside and not feeling as much as he knew he should, he realised that, if you stripped away the flesh, all a person comprised was a word, a name, a semantic entity that figured heavily in a number of intersecting narratives, the hero perhaps of its own and maybe even of others, but still in the end, only a word and thus subject to the same laws of vacancy as any other.

He kicked out at a pizza box on the floor and sent it skittering across the room, frightening the cat which ran for cover in the sepulchral darkness of the kitchen. If he'd been able to write just this one, last story then everything perhaps would have been alright. He could have re-emerged into the light like a creature from subaquatic hibernation feeling that he had plumbed the inky depths and returned with something gleaming in his hand, but in truth he felt as if the muse had deserted him, run off with another and left him only with dry, wrinkled prose, arid and sterile, word upon word, to show for his journey. Throwing himself onto the sofa and in doing so generating a mini-explosion of polystyrene and paper, he rattled the bus queue of cider cans at its side one by one, checking for uncontaminated contents and, finding one that felt relatively safe, took a long swig.

His eyes settled on the mound of objects in the centre of the room. Books without covers, ripped up magazines, the sleeves of albums, a telephone directory open at the pizza page. As he stared at them he felt something bother him, something like a small child pulling at his sleeve, outside his peripheral vision. He refocused his eyes to try and see what it was. There it was again, something about their configuration, order in the chaos. A phrase, five words, each coming from a different source but overlaid from the angle where he was sitting in such a way that they made a sentence. 'The Real Is The Impossible'. There was even a phrase underneath, an album title, that contained his name. He laughed, smirked at the ridiculousness of it, his clutter speaking to him, somehow ingeniously finding a voice. But what to make of the axiom? Had he heard it somewhere before? He took another pull on the cider only to realise from the splattering of the contents around his lips that his hand was shaking badly. As abruptly as it had come, the laughter of the previous moment died back, transmogrifying into something colder and more desiccated.

Yes, it was an intriguing coincidence, a random conjugation that by rights should not have been there, but at the same time, as he'd read it, he'd heard a voice, the first in over three weeks, and it had not been his own. It was uncanny, *unheimlich* in the language of psychoanalysis – like some nameless, oceanic horror erupting from the deep and breaking through the surface close by. At the thought, he found himself suddenly panicking, swallowing repeatedly, gulping on air as if the cider had formed into a bolus in his throat and was unwilling to move in either direction. He sat up abruptly, acutely aware that if he didn't breathe properly soon he would move into oxygen debt and from there to unconsciousness, feeling for the first time in years the intense pang of total isolation, almost hermetic insulation, from the society of others, of being face to face with an issue which is of consuming interest only to oneself. He stood up and staggered through the debris to the kitchen, knowing somehow instinctively that he had to get some clean, pure liquid, lots of it, down his throat, however hypothetical the obstruction, and as he took mouthfuls of the stuff and compressed it with his tongue into his oesophagus, he gradually felt the passageway clear and the crisis avert. By the end of it, he was left shaking, weakened, arms outstretched resting on the sink, eyes trying to make sense of the darkness. And that was when he saw it, resolving slowly like an internet image, a chain of words reading vertically, almost hieroglyphically down the objects in the sink, another apparent message: 'Why is Original Best?' He scrabbled at the items with his right hand, wanting to deny them their distributive logic, finding himself holding one by one a packet of coffee, a can of bitter, a bottle of whisky and a Listerine jar whose label had worn away in the water leaving just two letters behind. Once again, he had heard the peculiar, leaden voice in his head, slow and measured even as it framed the slightly ungrammatical interrogative. And what was worse, he even felt as if he was under some sort of compulsion to answer it.

For what was so special about the original, why did it have such a high value across, as far as he knew, all cultures all societies? He stared glumly down at the plughole, hoping somehow to find enlightenment there in the tangled mess of spaghetti and coffee grains. There was little to go on, so he returned to the question, letting his eyes drift slowly upwards until they rested on the floral chase-work of the blind.

What was it that a copy or an imitation lacked that an original possessed? Presence of some sort? An investment, an energy, something that added a unique ingredient to the mix of what was previously available and thereby moved things on? Whatever it was, it was a quantity that he felt he particularly lacked at that moment. Being original was something he had always found relatively easy until these last few years, and the loss of the facility seemed to be linked to his increasing transparency, his lack of solidity, his inability to be genuinely anything at all. And what of the origin itself from which the original proceeded? The phrase implied a singular source, but if so, was it internal or external to the being through which the truly innovative flowed. He suspected the latter, but then this implied some sort of god, a condition beyond the conditioned, an idea with which these days he had very little truck. That said, he had fallen out with the concept little by little over the years and it was quite possible to track his diminishing faith together with the gradual fading of his gift such that they mapped over each other like the trading figures of two departments in a failing company.

Maiden groped his way back into the heavy silence of the living room, sensitised now to the language of litter, and looked around him for any more felicitous combinations. He didn't have far to look. On the coffee table by the sofa, three splayed books and a leaflet intoned across their covers 'There Is No Other Of The Other'. How ludicrous, he thought. What an absurd proposition! Perhaps because the last term was a partially obscured version of the word, he couldn't help himself thinking of his mother whom he used to visit every fortnight in the hope of tempering her alcoholism with his own more controlled version. That had stopped when, one drunken night, she had draped her arms around him and suggested that they go to bed together. He knew it was just the drink and the loneliness, and that she would undoubtedly have forgotten all about it the next morning, but all the same he hadn't known what to say, and had chosen to ignore the whole thing, shutting it away in the junk room with all the other strange events that had marked his passage through life. Such as his father always wrapping his arm around his girlfriends' shoulders whenever they visited and steering them off without even greeting him at the door. Such as the late-night phone-calls from his mother after his death threatening to commit suicide in an already lifeless voice, telling him she had razors in the bathroom. Such as the night he had spent in the matron's flat of an otherwise derelict mental hospital, frightened because there were people outside the door who that day had shaved off all of his hair, people who were unprepared to show themselves but quite happy to creep menacingly around the outlying parts of the building. Yes, it had been original, and original is undoubtedly best.

Now when he looked around the room he saw that there were outlandish slogans everywhere: 'Reality Is Thought' in the refuse spilling from the fallen bin; 'Give Peas A Chance' pinned chaotically around the pinboard; 'K Is For Cataclysm' built haphazardly out of words and letters ripped from *The Metro*; 'Barcode The Sky' emblazoned almost hieratically across the steppes of a pile of books in the mire by his feet. The floors, walls and surfaces virtually shouted them out one after an other whilst the peculiar voice in his head continued only to murmur insistently, like a bored teacher addressing a recalcitrant pupil. Were they all really there? Or was he actually seeing patterns that his own mind was forming in advance and projecting onto the detritus? There were so many words present in the room, such a seething swamp of verbiage to choose from, that it was surely inevitable that there would be sensible-seeming sentences here and there. In addition, the silence in the room was by now so all-engulfing that it was not surprising that he was hearing voices, that words were having to be spoken by any means necessary. He wondered if he had somehow just reached the point at which isolation becomes unsupportable and the demand for society so overwhelming that it must be obeyed at all costs. Perhaps this is what schizophrenia is like, he thought stutteringly, the inevitable effect of becoming so cut off from others that objects become animated, words live and breathe and something like sense seems to break through everywhere you turn. If so, then perhaps he was actually going mad. It was a proposition that, despite everything, he had never before seriously considered and it made him long, more than anything, for a serious drink. But there was nothing but left-overs remaining in the flat. He would have to go out. For the first time in three weeks, he would have to open the front door and make the long, treacherous journey to the local off-license.

Maiden sat down by the computer and buried his head in his hands, pushing the palms hard into his eyes. In the ebb and flow of the blackness he half-imagined he saw the room as if from hundreds of feet above and it looked like a half-empty packing crate in a cellar, or some madman's idea of a dolls' house. Worse than that, it looked like a prison, a cell, something stifling, something that was about to seal over and incarcerate its puny occupant for all time. Certainly he had to admit now that his time was up, his seclusion over and the sixth and final story was still far from being completed. But perhaps that was the point – it could not be finished until he had broken the seal, the covenant that he had made with solitude, and opened the cell door, hand in hand with no one, aware for the first time of the true fragility of his being.

He looked up at the computer screen and reached for the mouse, intending to shut down his abortive story for the evening, only to be stopped mid-action by the juddering realisation that the last four words were not his own, had not been there before, and had thus appeared on the page entirely of their own accord. He was not even sure that they made sense. Could they be the truncated version of something that he had written earlier, a paragraph from which most of the words had become somehow deleted? Or had the machine itself, the software, glitched and thrown them up, vomited them out, as the effluvial by-product of an altercation between the zeroes and the ones? He didn't know, but there they were, stark, almost primordial in their simplicity: 'Nothing Is Not Itself'. Once again, the voice spoke as he read them, slowly and monotonously as before, but this time grinding them out as if for the hard of hearing. There was an air of menace about the enunciation, an air of fucking menace…

He was not having this. He was not having this at all. First the flat had spoken to him, random conjugations of terms, harmless, linguistic paradiddles, but now his computer was attempting to insinuate double negatives into his consciousness. What was nothing if it was not itself? Or did it mean that everything actually was itself i.e. self-identical, in which case why state it in such a twisted and perverse fashion? He shuddered, shook his shoulders and took a series of deep breaths to calm himself down. 'I'm just filling the silence,' he announced loudly, 'making things up to occupy the void!' The words trampled through the air like wellington boots in mud, each one disgorging itself as it made way for the next. All of a sudden, the heavily curtained windows, the graffitied walls and the littered floor seemed intensely oppressive and he knew that he only had seconds to get out, seconds before he had to re-engage with the world or disappear screaming somewhere inside himself.

He grabbed his wallet from the table and dived for the door, crushing a thousand species of can and carton underfoot as he went. Wrenching his coat down from the peg in the hall, he ran for the front entrance, preparing himself as best he could for the trauma of his reinsertion into the social, but before he could open the door he stopped. Stopped dead.

For lying on the mat there was a white envelope, a white envelope that he was sure had not been there before. He bent down and picked it up, noting the lack of inscription on the reverse as he did so. Slipping his finger inside the gap at the top, he ripped across and then shook out the contents onto the palm of his hand. It was a single sliver of paper, oblong, about three inches by five, with what appeared to be a set of instructions written in minute script on one side:

Don't Use Superlatives!
Avoid Passives!
No Clichés!
Watch Howevers and Buts!

They were a formalised version of his own rather weakly-applied commandments to himself and, what was worse, they were written in his own handwriting. Somehow, without knowing it, he had sent the message to himself. But if so, then surely that meant that there must be two of him, one of which was conveying itself to the other beyond its ken, outside of its control. The left hand no longer knew what the right hand was doing. He was a split-self. He stared down at his palms in horror, looking for any evidence, any sort of twitch or movement that would indicate autonomic functioning. In the hall mirror he checked his dishevelled image point by point, half-expecting the reflection to lose faith, peel itself away and walk off out of the frame. He was in trouble now, he realised that, much deeper trouble than he'd suspected. For if who he was and who he thought he was had parted company and the one now found it necessary to communicate with the other by sending it disembodied messages, then there wasn't a 'he' left in any simple sense, only something fractured and broken, something that perhaps opposed itself and would one day march off into a future of its own making. How far had he already gone down that road? What had he done? Where had he been?

As he stumbled back into the living room, he heard the familiar clunk of the printer next to his computer as it sucked in a sheet of paper and his heart sank. For God's sake! What was this? He hadn't set anything to print. Trampling through the garbage, he made his way across to it and waited nervously for the first sheet to begin to emerge. It was the beginning of a story, a story he had no memory of having written, something called 'Channel 3', and it was explicitly about himself. As the printer churned out the pages, he read, impossibly, the history of the last twenty minutes of his life somehow already converted into text, right up to the moment where he had tried to get out of the front door. Then the narrative diverged away from what had actually occurred and followed its own course. There was no envelope, no set of instructions, no looking in the mirror. Instead it reported a very different scenario, one that, as he read, Maiden or the part of him that was left couldn't help feeling with growing, nail-biting dread might actually represent the truth and leave him no exit, no means of escape:

All he was interested in was opening the door, getting out of the flat, being in the world once more. He had been blocked and lacking an outlet for too long, trapped in a body, effectively a carcass, that no longer responded to his desires. The time had come for him to break free, to prise apart the ligaments and strike out on his own. He turned the key and pulled, was about to hurl himself into the corridor when a surge of instinctive adrenaline stopped him in his tracks, the same biochemical response that would have prevented him from throwing himself forward into a stream of traffic. For the truth was that the corridor, the stairwell, the neighbour's front door were not there. In their place was only light, a soft, grey mantle like early morning mist that licked the edges of the door frame and stole across the threshold. Maiden gazed into it, into its dawning heart which seemed to offer at least some form of hope and – without a second thought for all that he was leaving behind – stepped out, became transparent and then was gone.

SEAN O'BRIEN

I Cannot Cross Over

After Antonio Tabucchi

'You don't want to go down there, pet,' she said, pausing in the mouth of the lane. 'Come in here for a nice drink with me.' Beyond her I could see the beer signs through the windows of the bar.

'Sorry but I can't,' I said. 'I'm supposed to be elsewhere.'

'What's that got to do with owt? Come on.'

The bells of the cathedral church began to toll, sending mass flights of starlings racing over the old town. The light was taking on the neon edge it gets at six o'clock in summer. It was the magic hour for freezing lager and pepper vodka.

'Sorry.'

'You won't get a better offer.'

'I know, it's just –'

'Suit yourself. Bloody poets.' And she was gone with a clatter of heels over the cobblestones. I couldn't remember how we'd fallen into conversation. Maybe walking down from the Metro station at Monument. Maybe she asked for a look at my paper. It didn't matter. I liked her with her piled up dyed blonde hair, I liked the frankness of her manner and her cleavage. But I had to be elsewhere. You know how it is, in the middle of things.

I turned off into Pudding Chare. What would her name be? I saw clearly – and maybe it was true – that she was called Lorraine and that by day she worked on a cosmetic counter in Fenwicks, wearing terra cotta make-up. It seemed a strangely romantic life to me at that moment, though doubtless filled with the normal obstructions and sadness.

As I hurried on I looked into the window of a bar round the back of the newspaper offices, a place once used by print workers. There was already half a crowd in there – blonde girls, their heads averted, none of them precisely her.

On the steps of the Lit and Phil Library I met Tommy the caretaker sweeping up the glass from a broken sherry bottle. Tommy was a naturalized Aberdonian. His expression always indicated that his suspicions were being confirmed.

'You're late the night,' he said.

'But not too late, I hope.'

He studied his watch.

'Well. No. But divvent fuck about. Miss Quine is long away and I want to get a good seat in the Innisfree. For the exotics.' He winked, like a lustful automaton. I imagined his female equivalent in her pinny and headscarf sliding stiffly out of the door behind him on her track, while he was drawn back into the darkness.

'I just need to check something.'

'Aye, well, it's a library,' he said, and turned back to his sweeping.

In the main gallery the three girls at the issue desk sat reading and fiddling with their long fair hair, perched on stools like mermaids on their rocks. None of them looked up as I passed – I could have been anyone – but I heard a faint echoing *tut* as I reached the doors at the far end. Was I a nuisance? I was a member. I went down the stone staircase, past paintings of the nineteenth century magistrates and antiquarians who had nurtured the library towards its present sepia perfection. None of these long-gone gentlemen would meet my eye just now.

The Silence Room is a place I do not care for. It is a brown chamber crowded with stacks of county records from the eighteenth and nineteenth centuries, as well as some impractically narrow tables at which anorexic pedants sometimes crouch to labour. It feels like an abandoned work by M.R. James. Bad enough on a spring evening when the light comes faintly down the crack between the library and the Coroner's Court and through the crusty window. Unthinkable on a foggy winter night.

All I knew was there was meant to be something in there for me to collect, perhaps a message. Where would you hide something in a library? Not among the books, surely. That could lead to misunderstanding: you might mistake a scribbled execration for the message. You could end up standing there, pondering the meaning of *nonsense* or *shite*.

I paced the parquet floor, wondering where to look. Fortunately the pedants had all gone home, leaving only the faintest tremor of disapproval. I felt beneath the tables each in turn, in case there was something stuck there with gum or worse. Nothing. But I couldn't simply leave: where would I go? I cast around, at a loss, then noticed, not for the first time, that the grille covering the radiator beneath the window had been loosened, as if in some incomplete act of maintenance or vandalism. Now I put my hand inside. The sudden heat shocked me. I was feeling awkwardly around when I heard a voice.

'Now then you dorty fucker. Get yer hand oot of its arse man.'

'What?'

'I'm not surprised yer fuckin deef neither.'

It was the poet Ralph Cowan. He was a drunk. In fact he was more of a drunk than a poet, though his real vocation was heckling. His jacket sagged to one side under the weight of a bottle. He brandished a ham and pease pudding sandwich in one hand; in the other he waved a sheet of paper.

'Yer looking fer this, reet.' Ralph was in his pomp.

'What is it?'

'Fucked if I knaa, canny lad.'

Suddenly indifferent, he handed me the paper. On it was

typed, 'I cannot cross over.'

'That's a quotation from the great storehouse of local song and story,' he said, examining his sandwich. 'As ye would knaa if ye was from round here.'

'I do know, Ralph.'

'Not properly. Wouldn't be possible that.'

I looked at the line of typing again. The typewriter ribbon was worn, with both the red and black strands showing through.

'Ye gannin fer a drink?'

'Not with you.'

'Ya cunt. Go on.'

'No thanks.'

'Go on, cunt. Call yerself a poet? Howay man, what about the republic of fuckin letters, man?'

'I'm busy. Let me through the door, Ralph. Don't make me knack you.' He stepped aside.

'Busy? Aye, writin more daft radio shite about Collingwood's monument. Aboot which ye knaa fuckin fuck all by the way.' He followed me halfway up the stairs. 'No need to be stand-offish, like.'

Back in the gallery I could hear the drumming of rain on the glass dome above. How quickly the weather had changed. Seeing Ralph's familiar brown hooded mackintosh on the coat stand by the coffee hatch, I slipped it on and left without a second glance.

When I came out on to the street I had a sudden sense of the urgency of my situation. Wherever I was meant to go, and for whatever purpose I was meant to go there, I needed to be making better progress. Now there was torrential rain, with thunder unrolling overhead. Crowds of girls in next to nothing ran shrieking over the road between hydroplaning taxis. A drayman's horse had been struck by lightning and lay smoking and hissing on a zebra crossing while its owner stamped and raved in the flooded gutter and passengers flooding from the railway station rushed past with umbrellas and briefcases raised like the accused on their way into court. A police car nosed slowly through the crush. I thought: I must write it all down when I get chance.

In this town everything gravitates towards the Quayside, so I decided to let physics take its course. But then as I made for the steps beside the ruined castle keep I saw the lights of the bar at the entrance to the high bridge. I didn't want to drink with Ralph Cowan, but I could certainly do with a refreshing beverage. And perhaps, with chance to reflect, my thinking would be clarified. Once through the doors, though, the signs were bad. The place was heaving with lawyers talking at the tops of their voices. I ordered a pint of stout and took a seat in the brown mirrored gloom of a bay as far as possible from the crowd.

What now? I thought. I could simply sit there and smoke cigarettes and drink beer on the off chance that something would happen. Waves of new lawyers came in, loud with triumph and worldly wisdom. Gradually they spilled backwards from the bar area, preening and jabbering until all I could see were their expensive corvine backsides. I looked down in despair. Under my glass was a crudely printed leaflet. I examined it. *Poetry Workshop*, it said. *Upstairs, tonight.*

I couldn't remember how long ago it was since last I climbed the sticky treads of that narrow staircase. The memory was both immediate and remote, like a first visit to the dentist. There was a sweet sick smell of beer and smoke. At the first turning I nearly collided with a woman in a red PVC raincoat. She pushed past me, putting on a pair of sunglasses, weeping, swearing under her breath. It was always a hard school, I thought, but tonight's workshop could barely have got started.

I slipped through the door and peered through the pall of smoke in the Function Room. A dozen participants of all

117

ages sat with bowed heads at the little tables, writing furiously on lined pads. At the front of the group stood Walter Demarest, high priest of the Beginners' Group – a gaunt grey man with an eyepatch and a thermos flask. It was, he gave people to understand, his manifest destiny to issue weekly disappointments to his obedient secular flock. They would thank him in the end. He had a plate in his head.

'You can't come in,' he said. 'You're not a member.' Then, recognizing me, he muttered, 'Got summat for you.' He began to search one of the many carrier bags of manuscripts and magazines and small press publications which surrounded his table. 'Brought it with me, I know that.'

'What is it?'

'In a manila envelope.' He continued ferreting. Everyone had stopped to watch. Some of them took the chance to dab their faces with Kleenex. 'Got it,' Walter said at last. He handed me a stiff seven by five manila envelope. Nothing was written on it. The group waited.

'Open it, then,' said someone.

'How do I know it's for me?'

'She told me it was,' said Walter.

'Who did?'

'Dunno. Some French bird. Blonde.'

Not French, I thought, but Belgian. Zsa Zsa Maeterlinck. At last.

'We haven't got all day,' said Walter. 'We're only booked till eight.'

I opened the envelope. Inside was a single black garter trimmed with red.

'O-ho!' said someone.

'Best be off,' I said.

'Aye,' said Walter. 'Some of us have got poems to write.'

By now a heavy fog had rolled in up the river. The traffic tiptoed off the bridge and the drunks tiptoed under the traffic. I don't know why, but I felt my way along a wall of glazed white brick until I found a gap and skated down a cobbled alleyway into a back court surrounded by stooped and ancient solicitors' offices. Only the stairwells were lit now, their grades of desolation rising to the dim yellow spaces under the roofs, where the lifts turned back and the cares of innumerable forgotten lives lay stacked in brown folders, awaiting the attentions of rot. This was something else I was going to have to get round to writing about, afterwards, whenever that might be.

Melancholy overtook me now. I could taste the fog, as though I were breathing through the woollen scarf my mother had made me wear as a child. It had a stony, watery, acrid taste. It was like something official which everyone had mistakenly assumed was long gone into exile. It was like the first day at school. I felt afraid.

Another entryway led me into a street with flooded gutters, running beneath the viaduct, a place of informal archway garages and erotic assignations conducted on a similar economic basis. The yellow doorway of a pub leered out of the gloom, so I went in. The bar was empty, but there was the loud steady noise of many voices somewhere in the building. Behind the bar a calendar showed Miss September, Zsa Zsa Materlinck wearing a smile and a garter. I noticed that the year she represented contained only nine months. Time was pressing.

'Private party,' said the florid, brilliantined manager, emerging through the smoke, his tooth glinting to match his tiepin. He twirled a gold Albert hanging on a chain from his waistcoat, and nodded towards the hatch. 'Funeral, like. Stout, is it?'

A barmaid with a face like a large red fish in a beehive hairdo leaned through the hatch.

'We need some more crabsticks, Maurice,' she said.

'What do they fockin dee with 'em aal?' the gaffer said. 'Have you ever seen anyone actually eating one?' he asked me.

I tried to look noncommittal. But really I knew where the crabsticks went – down the cracks of the plush benches at funeral buffets.

'Whose do is it?'

'Dennis Foot. Ye knaa him?'

'I know of him.' Dennis Foot was the legendary angling correspondent of the *Argus*. He too had been a poet. And now he was gone to his long home. Or perhaps they would bury him at sea, or burn him like a Viking. I struggled to find anything to add to this thought. Call yourself a poet?

Eventually I asked, 'What did he die of?'

'Seafood poisoning,' said the manager. 'Never touch it meself like.'

The barmaid came through with a new tray of crabsticks.

'Go on, pet, since you're here.'

'I'm a vegan.'

'We're very broadminded. Hang on. You're him. Aren't you?'

'Perhaps I'm not the person you should ask.'

'I've gorra note from your pal.'

I couldn't remember having any pals. I couldn't remember being in this pub, or this pub being here before.

'The skinny one. Wears a coat.' She took a betting slip from her bosom and handed it to the manager. He looked at me carefully, then put on a pair of spectacles and read the note:

'The river is wide but I cannot.' What's that supposed to mean, like?'

'Hard to say.'

'Sounds bloody daft,' said the barmaid. 'Vegan, right?' She exchanged glances with the manager.

'I could show you me poems if you want, like', he said, shyly.

'Actually I'm a bit pressed now.'

He carefully took off his spectacles and re-pocketed them in his waistcoat.

'Word to the wise,' he said.

'Of course.'

'Yer barred.'

Back in the fogbound night a coal train crawled past, high overhead, adding its rusty black sweat to the fog. Press on, I thought. The viaduct curved away and quiet fell. Now the street was edged with metal fencing topped with razor wire. I had heard of this place but never visited it before. The Cultural Quarter. A gate stood open. I picked my way across the rubble and rags to a low concrete building which felt as if it stood at the edge of a cliff. It was the kind of place the army would have used as a venereal clinic. In fact it was the premises of a publisher. The door swung open. So this was my pal. Neville Stone.

'Been a while,' he said, extending a cold white hand from the overlong sleeve of his dark overcoat.

'I wasn't expecting you,' I said. 'I thought you were dead.'

'That's rather an emotive term,' said Neville. He offered me his hipflask. I declined. As he tipped his head back there came the faint pang of vodka, not a smell, just a rumour, one for the columns of Intimations in the *Argus*. Neville led me inside. The front office contained nothing but old catalogues. The storeroom held only old ladder-style shelving. Beyond both lay the editor's office. This too was empty, except that in the middle of the floor stood a wooden pallet bearing several stacks of shrink-wrapped calendars. One package had been ripped open. Neville handed me a sample. Zsa Zsa was still smiling. The garter, I now saw, was part of a pre-Christmas theme, matching her hat.

'So what happened? Where's all the poetry?'

'Pulped. Turned into these.' He flicked through the slick pages. The muses addressed their compliant smirks to eternity.

'The culture turned against us, that's what. Or the economy. Or both. Or they're the same. Or something.

Anyway, there was no call for these either.'

'All a bit valedictory.' I said.

'You what? We're past all that.'

I looked at the calendar. Miss May in her green scarf reached across the void to Zsa Zsa, her September cousin.

'No chance of any royalties, anyway,' said Neville, looking at his watch. 'It would appear the guvnor's fucked off. Fancy a drink?

'I've got to be somewhere.'

'That's what they all say. Where are you headed?'

'The quayside, I think. That's where I've been trying to get to all night.'

'Ahuh? I'll come down with you.'

It was sleeting through the fog as we picked our way down the steps between the wrecked nineteenth century warehouses beloved of alkies and the producers of costume dramas about the nobility of toil. Fires burned in a few rooms half-open to the air. Dim figures reclined and howled or held out brown bottles which we politely refused.

'You're ready then,' said Neville, as we reached the foot of the steps, where the bass-heavy judder of music could be heard.

'Am I?'

'Why else would you be here?'

'I'm not with you.'

'Then why'd you come?' He shook his head.

'Am I supposed to know?'

At last we came out on the street. It was crowded with the usual drinkers, groups and singletons passing silently through the music along the potholed road, slowing the night traffic along the quays. Faces I knew raised bottles in recognition and moved expressionlessly on. The sleet had turned to snow, the broad slow flakes landing on the men's bald heads and the women's naked shoulders

'I'll leave you here,' said Neville. He hailed a girl who

stood in the red doorway of a bar. She waved back and went inside.

'What am I meant to do?' I asked.

He shrugged, shook my hand coldly again, then slipped over the road as the crowd thickened about him.

I let myself be drawn along with the drinkers. An eddy carried me to the river's edge, where I stopped to lean on the railings and looked down into the black waters. They were high tonight. The tide was running swiftly away, parting smoothly at the high bridge-pillars, bearing a mass of branches aloft like antlers. Among the branches, pages from the calendar surfaced – all Zsa Zsa – and were snatched below. Then, slowly, but without slowing, the water grew smooth as a mirror. My face appeared in it, with the moon on one shoulder and another face to balance it. I spoke to the figure in the water.

'You don't live here.'

'I don't live anywhere. That's the trouble, son.' The figure drew deeply on a cigarette and breathed out smoke into his white hair.

'Well, I can't help you now.'

'I know that, son,' my father said. 'Nor I you.'

'Why does it have to be you?'

He smiled bitterly. I saw the handsome devil he had been.

'Perhaps it's an ordeal.'

'Ordeals are normally rewarded,' I said.

'Are they? Are you sure? Then perhaps I'm your reward. Walk with me anyway.' He turned and threw his cigarette into the water. But when I looked up there was no one beside me. The crowds had thinned out, too. The swing bridge was open and stragglers made their way up the approaches. The waters stood still as a sealed pool, in perfect black silence. There was no sound of voices, no breaking glass, no distant traffic in the streets above the quays. The music had ended, and one by one the lights along the quay went out. I looked around for my father, for Neville, for any companion to come with me over the bridge. All gone.

'It can't be as important as this, whatever it is,' I said.

By the time I stepped onto the bridge there was only the moon's cold lamp, with a face I liked to think was Zsa Zsa Maeterlinck's, with the snow falling into the water, and by this light I saw quite clearly that this was a river with only one side.

Tabs

The printed notice on the big table at the far end of the library was so discreet you might have thought it referred to something mundane, like the Easter closing hours – the kind of information the members acquired by osmosis anyway. In fact it stated that from March 31st – 'in line with trends elsewhere in society in general' – smoking would be banned in the library.

Change and decay in all around I see. Surely, though, the library wasn't subject to the same processes and historical forces as 'elsewhere'. It was the *library*: an ancient institution where you had to pay a subscription to join, supposing the committee's inquisitors judged you fit for membership. If all went well and you got past the caretaker and up the stone stairs you were safe in 1964, or 1958, or, if you preferred, 1913, when all the world smoked. The authority of 'elsewhere' was suspended: that was the point. *Smoking*, and smoking-affiliated activities like sitting around, like waiting, like passing the time between one thing finished and the next beginning – these, not reading and writing, gave the library its *raison d'être*. It was a smoking library – damn few others like it anywhere. And now the lights were going out all over Europe.

There had been a time when the smoking ban would have meant a row. There would have been resignations and calls for extraordinary meetings. And, though it would have made no difference to the outcome, there would have been impassioned mutterings around the big table. This was the headquarters of a *salon des refusés* of the law and the academy.

This shifting group of desperate men clung to the idea of house-ownership and the life of the mind by their fingertips there at the smoky hub of the library, like Balzacian gamblers leaving the wheel of their ruined fortunes only to drink and to pawn their last possessions. The fraternity of the big table passed the days by looking at the nudes in *Practical Photography*, rolling cigarettes and writing endless letters of application to ever more obscure law firms and institutions of higher education. Their low chorus of dissent served as a reassuring background, however far away you sat. Even in the remote monastic setting of the Silence Room in the sub-basement among the county archives they could be heard, like a warning in a foreign language. Now, I realized, they too were gone, somehow – never noticed them go – and in a week or two smoking would be gone as well. The library was much too quiet.

What would remain, at least for a time, were the oily encrustations which had grown slowly, like black reefs of disease, over the books shelved in the upper galleries. You could find all sorts up there where the poets went to die – early Auden, MacNeice, Empson, alongside historical curiosities with local connections like Michael Roberts (Longbenton) and Francis Scarfe (South Shields). There was even, mysteriously, an original 1923 edition of Wallace Stevens's *Harmonium*: upstairs, it sweated tar like Eliot's Thames. By and large the diseased yellow air of these autumnal upper galleries was the haunt of librarians. They shifted the smoke-ruined stock from shelf to shelf, like nineteenth century doctors sending their doomed consumptive patients from spa to spa. Among the sufferers were Mann's *The Magic Mountain* and Katherine Mansfield's stories – sick books that no one read now or cared to be reminded of, shunted off to heaven's gate and replaced by crime novels and lite lit for lowbrow ladies. It is of course unfair to associate the decline of smoking with the death of the educated general reader: after all, one is a fact and the other merely a suspicion, and all they have in common is simultaneity. But still. – Anyway, the chances were you could get hold of the Wallace Stevens if you cared to ascend the wrought-iron spiral staircase into the previous century. Then, one day, *Harmonium* wasn't there.

It was down on the big table, it turned out, lying unopened next to a packet of tobacco, some licorice Rizlas and a lighter the shape of a u-boat conning tower. The saturnine Harry Box was looking at the book as he rolled a cigarette. He continued to look at the book as he lit the cigarette. He renewed his scrutiny as he exhaled the first drag.

'Are you using that?' I asked.

'Ahuh.'

'I mean the copy of *Harmonium*.'

'Ahuh.'

I picked up the *TLS* and waited. A couple of years later, he glanced up and said: '*Fill your black hull / With white moonlight. // There will never be an end / To this droning of the surf.*' He seemed to expect a reply.

'Stevens.'

'Course it is.'

'From *Harmonium*.'

'Course it is.'

There seemed to be no way forward from here. Harry looked a shade disappointed.

'Tell you what.'

'Yes?'

'It's fuckin' mint, mind. Whatever any cunt says.'

To the best of my knowledge, no cunt had disparaged Stevens lately. It took me a moment to recognize, in the present context, an example of the pre-emptive aggression, directed at imagined slights, which characterizes this fascinating part of the country. Honour satisfied, Harry rose and put his papers into his carrier bag, along with the copy of *Harmonium*, then left the building. He did not stop to check the book out at the issue desk. *Harmonium* may have been the property of the library, but it was Harry Box who really owned it. When I had used the book before, it had merely been on loan from Harry. I was intrigued.

Harry Box was sometimes physically in, but never professionally *of*, the Applicants Anonymous group at the big table. For one thing he had a job – some undefined lecturing post at a college south of the river – politics or history, I never knew exactly. Attired in his patented gloom, wearing the aromatic pall of his steady consumption, he continued to quote Stevens spontaneously from time to time over the next few years. These occasions were like Bank Holidays in a Trappist monastery. *Ramon Fernandez, tell me if you can…The world is ugly and the people are sad…Upon a hill in Tennessee.* He delivered a line, then seemed to listen to it fading in time, smiling through his smoke as if it pleased him that this was the case. Thus we approached the Millennium – the ageing youths and Harry and myself, riding the table like a raft while storms elsewhere consumed unlucky mariners by the shipload.

Like many men of a certain age, out in the badlands, a few years short of forty, Harry made a big performance of the hand-rolled cigarette. He made it into an *activity*. For the duration of the making, until he nipped off a couple of loose threads of *Old Hawser*, or whatever he was smoking that week, you believed him: this was the preface to something decisive; a deed was imminent, of which all this fadge was simply the herald. Rolling a cigarette was more than a way of occupying the meantime; it was substantial and meaningful behaviour. It spoke for a world, the one at which Harry gestured through the smoke as he breathed it out in rings: the world of Stevens and the library, the bridges and the river that ran darkly beneath them, of the river's mouth and the vast satisfactory distances beyond, from here to either pole and on to Singapore and Valparaiso. Even Harry's moustache was involved in the smoke somehow, and thus in that wider world where the atlas was mainly blue, where yawning depths were crossed by vessels with Harry's rolling tobacco secreted in their bilges, like contraband. God, the man could smoke.

One day he put an open book down on the table in front of me.

'Look at that.'

I read where his yellow finger pointed: *Take a last turn / In the tang of possibility.*'

'That's what I mean,' he said. 'Do you know what I mean?'

'I think so.'

'I wanted to be a ship's navigator. I took the vision test. Turned out I was colour blind.' He smiled through the smoke, closed the copy of Heaney's *Wintering Out* and went back to reading Stevens. You could feel the globe waiting, still patient, for someone to cross it, for Harry to give up his self-possession and simply *go*. Colour blindness was only a setback. There were other means of travel. *Tout est luxe, calme et volupté.* Surely there was time. I was anxious for Harry's sake that this should be the case: anxious, I mean, that the imagination should be vindicated in its travels. For around the same time, equally unexpectedly, he showed me a handful of poems.

Normally this is a signal to make one's excuses and leave, if necessary starting a new life in a different part of the country. Beware of trespassing in the realm of green ink and alternative spelling, where the obsessed are waiting to waylay you with their lives' work. But Harry's poems were interesting. They drew on the Baudelaire of 'Le Voyage', on Rimbaud and Conrad and RLS and other seagoing literature of all kinds – and of course on Stevens, who, like Harry, never went anywhere, certainly never Abroad. Harry had Stevens's feel for the exotic. He could find it in the dancers – 'exotics' with the glottal 't' – in the clubs on Shields Road on Sunday lunchtimes, where Stevens probably would not; but

Harry also understood the power of names: Tehuantepec, Valparaiso, Far Cathay, planted like a path of islands, further and further into the ocean. (*Where mind and ocean meet.* I realized that where other people had conversation, Harry had quotation and reference.) The combination of longing and pre-emptive disappointment had something of Laforgue about it, but at bottom it was all his own. It was as if in any encounter he had always just cast off, back into the smoke-filled Sargasso of his seemingly unshakeable preoccupations, steered by the self-possession whose one command was *not yet*; *manana*. His mode of conversation was always, I see now, the farewell.

We fell into the habit – I'm not sure exactly how or when – of drinking together on Wednesdays when the library closed early. We crossed the river by the High Level Bridge to sit among the resonant desolation and imminent violence of the Coffin Bar. We re-crossed the water to perform what Harry called 'a sector crawl', along the quayside as the developers took aim at its dozen old blokes' bars, or wandered up behind the hospital and into the fringes of the West End, where wise men always went equipped but literary types were safe because ignored. Our conversation was simple, repetitive and – to me – intensely pleasurable. It took in Wallace Stevens, Baudelaire, Rimbaud, modernism and the sea. Harry, I recognize now, said very little. He would launch a sentence, a quotation, an allusion, down the slipway of the evening and watch as it drifted from view. The evenings dissolved like smoke in the contemplation of fragments and gnomic *aperçus*. It was with Harry that I developed a taste for Scotch, a dark mild made from the scrapings of ashtrays and the urine of smokers. When we were getting drunk, Harry would say, 'Out there, out there,' gesturing at the bar-room door or the gantry or the dartboard, but meaning the ocean, the immense, the sublime, the all-consuming dimension where the mind could drink, drown and be re-born at eternal leisure. The riches of those absconders' hours! Sometimes a withered glass collector in a Cyrenians' suit would nod agreement at one of Harry's sudden announcements and suddenly tell us that he had been regimental bantamweight champion, that he had caught a spectacular disease in Port Said, that he had fathered a child on a black woman in Durban and always meant to go back. Harry would nod: here was proof of all he intended. He would roll the man a cigarette and then suddenly we would be out in the street, walking briskly despite being half-cut. When I asked why, Harry would say: 'He's that unhappy.'

Harry was engaged, it seemed, to a primary school teacher, Anne. She remained a misty, notional figure. She was never the direct subject of his discourse: she only emerged as sort of grammatical necessity, with consequences for other kinds of statement, referred to in terms of having to go home eventually from whichever pub we had arrived in when the library closed. Relations between the sexes seemed almost unrevised hereabouts in those days: men were selfish and women complained. It took a long time for people to realize that they could manage these roles independently. When they finally did, almost overnight entire streets ceased to have a male population. A female quiet of afternoon television commenced, broken only by the weekend departures of children with overnight bags. You saw them climbing into cars whose drivers preferred not to approach the house.

But that is to anticipate. Anne was a distant, more or less benevolent idea. I imagined her as a grown-up Grace Darling, ready in her mackintosh on playground duty to do the right thing if called upon. Even though I scarcely met her, like Harry she seemed in some way already historical, a beckoning figure in the rainy doorway of the Bridge or the Crown Posada or the Barking Dog, there to extract her man, with weary good humour, from the smoke-filled room of his choice and – dare one say it – his real affections.

'She seems nice,' I said.

'Aye, canny.'

Of course, we know nothing of other people's relationships, not really: so we tell ourselves. So I told myself that Harry's taciturn Geordismo was simply that, not an evasion of me (why need he bother? We were simply drinking companions), still less of his own life and of Anne. The mood I glimpsed between them was never of entrapped sadness on his part or of equally entrapped hopefulness on hers. Ignore that clock: the kind of time it marked was not the sort that Anne and Harry lived in. How could it be? The world was furnished with Stevens and Baudelaire – though admittedly I never found out what Anne preferred to read, supposing she did (there are people who – this is unimaginable, isn't it? – get by very well with scarcely a thought for language).

Anyway, Anne was to remain someone I never quite met. Although she came to fetch Harry several times, we were barely even on terms of glancing recognition when she disappeared back into the city to which she was, if anything, even more wedded than Harry was. If there was a problem, which of course there wasn't, it was that Harry was never wedded to her.

The problem was the other woman. I met her half a dozen times before I realized she *was* the other woman and not a colleague of Harry's or a friend of Anne's. Natalie would turn up in the pub or just happen to be there when we arrived. The contrast with Anne was so glaring as to be invisible, if you see what I mean. Where Anne was a pale, slight pastoral figure who should have been running a school for twelve children in the depths of Northumberland, Natalie was a creature of the city – a stilettoed blonde with crackling nylons and a voice like an icepick. Where Anne stood for patience, Natalie was all business, here, now and the next thing. Anne didn't smoke; Natalie favoured some blue-skinned, gold-tipped breed of tabs. They seemed to manufacture themselves in her tiny white handbag, into which she had evidently poured the entire contents of Wicksteeds' perfume department, where, I was not surprised to learn, she was employed in a supervisory capacity which seemed to involve standing about in a significant manner. I was only surprised that Harry should know her. She didn't strike me as a reader. Perhaps they had been at school together. Harry seemed, insofar as one could read these things, happy enough to see her. He would offer her a roll-up. She would shake her head and go on talking.

Natalie's world was full of doors she was just about to open, leading to further perfumed chambers and further exciting doors, and so on – a kind of opium dream of perpetual product launches, designed by Yves St. Laurent and Revlon. She was never stopping, only looking in, about to have to go to some unnamed but musky, darkly glittering venue. Yet her brief appearances were extremely flexible *vis-à-vis* the clock: Elizabeth and Helena and Coco and the rest clearly didn't mind being kept waiting. At the end of the night, when the city had once more turned into a zoo and I was aiming myself at the gaping hell-mouth of the Metro steps, Natalie would be talking about going on the Boat. The lure of this defunct cruise ship parked in the river escaped me. It has a revolving dancefloor and a legendary smell of sick. I left them to it. It is only now, in the deserts of Afterwards, that I make the connections: between Natalie and Jeanne Duval, Baudelaire's mysterious odalisque; between the local reputation of the staff of Wicksteeds' cosmetic department as part-time but vastly skilled courtesans and the cloying, imprisoning Parisian demi-monde which was the obverse of the infinite imagined ocean. Natalie was banging Harry's brains out.

Not knowing there was a crisis, I left Harry to it. Not that he would have asked for help or counsel. Not that I could have offered either. Aside from his genetic disinclination to talk about such things, our companionship was established on the basis of literary speculation. Life – that is to say, choice, responsibility, consequences – could not be permitted to intrude. That went without saying. You might object: how typically male, to overvalue – what? The pristine condition of something that in most circles would barely have qualified as conversation – *and to do so in defiance of a summons from life itself, i.e. Anne and / or Natalie.* How little you know, dear reader, if that is your view. Is there to be no space left for idleness and dreams, for the old boys' El Dorado? The Cythera of cancelled futurity?

I think, now, that Harry scarcely recognized his predicament: it was just how things went on, in the permanent meantime. But change was at hand. I noticed during the autumn that he was smoking readymades: Bensons, Silk Cut, nameless brands from backstreet minimarts – all of which he had previously treated with a hand-roller's studied contempt. He was lighting another before the first was finished. More than once I saw him look in disgusted bafflement at what he was smoking. How had things come to this, that life prevented him making his weekly visit to the bespoke tobacconist near the pawnbroker's shop to refurbish his supplies of Old Sumatra or Celebes Select? With the decline in the quality of smoking, so the ocean of his literary contemplations began to shrink.

There was nothing I could say. Harry's time – his world – was no longer his own, it seemed. He developed a hacking cough and struggled to mount Dog Leap Stairs on the way up from the quayside. He was often absent from the library. He altered then failed to keep drinking arrangements, or turned up very late, flustered, gasping, speechless. He staggered into the library one night, already well served by the look of him. He lowered himself into his usual seat at the big table and produced a silver hip-flask from an inside pocket. I declined the proffered shot. He emptied the flask, lit a Berkeley, put his head in his hands and said, in a voice I had never heard before, a voice from *outside* the library: 'Baudelaire's *Intimate Journals*, right? 'Today I felt myself brushed by the wing of madness.' I should fuckin coco. I'm fucked, man. That's the top and bottom of it. Fucked. The fuckin bitches have fuckin fucked me. Dunno where I am. Lost with all fuckin hands. Time to make smoke and disguise the heading. The Black fuckin spot's on its way. '

For a moment I was so startled I could not tell where the quotation ended and Harry began. I remember sitting there at the ashy table with my pen poised over the *TLS* crossword. This was a final leavetaking. Harry's world was being stripped of its rhetorical furnishings. All that remained was a bare unhappiness, about which there was nothing – forgive me, Tolstoy – to be said. Harry nodded, as if reading my thoughts.

'I'll catch you in the library,' he said, and walked away. Not until I heard the door swing shut did I look up. *We live, as we dream, alone.* A literary education is a wonderful thing: you need never be at a loss for the *mot juste.*

What happened next was unclear. From what I can gather, Harry went down to the Quayside, though no one knows what he had in mind. It was a snowy night. It seems that when he got to an empty stretch beyond the Baltic Mill there was someone, a woman, there before him, and that this person climbed over the railings and flung herself into the river. Harry hurled a lifebelt after her, to no avail, then ran to the nearest pub to phone for the emergency services. All this I got from the barman, later.

Having made the call, Harry ordered a double and – I think a lot about this – carefully rolled himself a cigarette. He drank the whisky and smoked his tab at leisure until a siren came into earshot, after which he left the building with several other punters and stepped off the pavement, just in time to be mown down by the ambulance.

As you may imagine, I have subjected these pitiful events to lengthy scrutiny. You will understand that I have searched for evidence of order, purpose, irony, comeuppance – in short, for meaning of any kind. I have to tell you that I have made no headway whatever. The bare succeeding facts are these. The woman was never found, despite the sustained efforts of the river police. Anne and Natalie were both safe and well. Harry acquired a plate in his leg and one in his head. He is said to have renounced poetry and moved to Middlesbrough where he occupies himself in some way I have not discovered, minus the company of either woman.

What a hopeless thing a fact can be, a mere dead weight of the actual. But we must work with what we have. People. Their (eventually) obvious sadness. Apparently it must be enough to discover all the merely contingent, wholly unmemorable human *mess* all over again, in papery dribs and drabs like this. Life may not amount to much: it certainly does not amount to literature, to the poems of *Harmonium* and *Les Fleurs du Mal*. Once I would kill for a book. Now I prefer to sit. I do not visit the library often, but when I do I find myself turning the pages of *Practical Photography*, wondering at the terrible unwitting power of the compliant demi-goddesses who lie in wait, there in the smoky light of those badly-imagined bordellos.

I reject this glum diminuendo! Let Harry disappear in style.

I see now that disappointment is a sort of fidelity, that for some people in some places defeat itself can be a virtue if treated with due reverence. Who is to say where disappointment springs from? But we can witness the process of its nurture all about us. The abolition of smoking in the library represents, I see now, what Harry and many others like him knew was bound to happen: not only would their ambitions be unfulfilled, their pleasures would be judged unacceptable. The world – if not Anne, then Natalie, if not her then some other damn thing – the world would be having them. The stupidity of the individual fate would be as irrelevant to this process as to everything else. One day they would look round and discover themselves to be anachronisms in a sense which had little to do with age. As a class, they were to be displaced into the realm of retired facts and foreclosed possibilities. They would take their bitterness with them as a badge of membership, but they would also have the immense, unending satisfaction of having achieved a final unshakeable immobility in which their worst suspicions were both confirmed and celebrated. Harry and his like would achieve their triumphant vindication. They would nod, roll a cigarette, exhale their smoke and vanish from sight. Harry would cease to take up the copy of *Harmonium* or Scarfe's translation of *Les Fleurs du Mal* while the great clock above the library doors unpicked the afternoon stitch by stitch. He would exit, at his own pace, from the library into nowhere, still smoking.

I have not myself smoked for many years, nor written a word till now, but with my task finished and the library at any moment about to close the doors on the world that gave it birth, I feel like lighting up just once more, for the enigmatic hell of it. *Luxe, Calme et Volupté: Tobacconists.*

The Custodian

I am a harmless drudge of the kind Dr Johnson described in
his *Dictionary*; not in fact a lexicographer like the great man
himself, but a toiler on the lower slopes of literature and
scholarship; an unearther of facts; a provider of notes and a
raiser of queries; a pedant with a heart of buckram. At
twenty-one I wrote poetry; at thirty-five I quibbled. You will
hear from people like me occasionally in the pages of the
Times Literary Supplement, putting a professor right on some
nearly invisible but – of course – fundamental detail. My
representative will be sitting at the back of the conference
hall, an unaffiliated scholar, demure but implacable, raising
an especially knotty textual point at the time of the afternoon
when everyone secretly wants to go home and read a
detective story. I held no post, no Fellowship, but none
doubted my right to the argument: who else would have
taken such recondite matters to heart in that lost world where
institutions were few and scholarship was still at least in part
the province of the modest gentleman?

My point is this: knowing what I know, after all these years
chained to the library, how would I sum myself up? Well, I
would say that I am interested in the possession of literature,
and in libraries; or, more simply, in possession.

I remember as if it were yesterday the morning I came
out of the rain and fog of the late 1940s, up the steps of the
library as usual, pausing to watch a tradesman painting a
new name at the bottom of the list of Presidents of the
Library. Eldon Wooler had died at eighty; the King was dead;
he was to be replaced in the year of our lord 1949 by

Derwent Rookhope: long live the Priest-King of the ancient library. The rule of the lawyers continued. Of this I say nothing except that I could never have been President, lacking the feral political talents required even in that narrowly specialized sphere. I was a merely a reader; a taker of notes; a quibbler, as you can hear.

Through the swing doors the library continued as usual – fog under the great domes, shuddering radiators, idlers browsing and smoking among the journals at the round table, the coffee-hatch redolent of the vivifying roast, though short of coffee in those austere times when only cold and virtue were freely available. To work, I thought, and passed through the double doors, and down a further set of broad stone steps, past Marmite-coloured portraits of Victorian worthies and into the specialized gloom of the basement where my papers were, by unstated agreement, permanently set out on a desk in the Silence Room. As I reached the foot of the stairs, Quinn, the caretaker, appeared in the doorway of the washroom, carrying a mop and bucket and smoking a cigarette forbidden down here. Fifty-odd, ten years my senior, the ruined creature nodded at me bitterly, half in challenge. This I ignored, passing through the black doors of the Silence Room and into my kingdom.

The Silence Room, whose name is self-explanatory, is not large, no larger than the front room of a large townhouse in Jesmond. Its floor is the original parquet. It contains a dozen wooden book-stacks, twelve feet high, in two rows divided by a central aisle. The stacks accommodated what might be called the senile elements of the library – local matters, of interest to antiquaries like myself and, thank God, to no one else. My speciality was – is – the poetic tradition of the region; here were my sources, here my happiness, the great, ignored work of scholarly synthesis that could never be completed. Around the walls were tall, glass-fronted cases containing vast volumes of county archives – land sales, things of that sort – dating back to the seventeenth century, waiting then, and waiting now, to be transferred to a more suitable location. I am not, as they say, holding my breath. Between the stacks, facing the walls, are small sloping desks for the use of scholars. In twenty years I could not remember seeing anyone else in the room other than Quinn and the implacable silver-haired librarian, Miss Greenwell, separately pursuing their silent ends. Into these I did not enquire. This was the Silence Room. It meant what it said; or rather, what it did not.

At that time my work concerned the manuscript of a strange eighteenth century text called *A Hexhamshire Tragedy*. This – as you may know? No matter – is a recasting of *King Lear* along the banks of the Tyne. In contrast to some other re-writings of Shakespeare, *A Hexhamshire Tragedy* maintains and even intensifies the horrors of the original. Indeed, by the end of Act Five so many corpses fill the stage that it is left to a hitherto non-speaking servant to sum up and bring down the curtain on this charnel-house of family romance. Interesting, no? My task was to compare this full text with another, incomplete version, apparently of similar date, called *A Tragedy of Killingworth*, in order to determine, if possible, which was the earlier work and publish the fact in the relevant journal. It would be stretching a point to claim that either piece, written anachronistically in late Jacobean blank verse, contained much of strictly literary merit; but if questions of value had been my primary interest I would never have entered the Silence Room all those years ago, would I?

As is my habit I worked steadily until one o'clock, then took my sandwiches to St Andrews churchyard on Darn Crook, there to ponder the resemblance of the rear of the premises overlooking the burial ground to the more famous Howff in Dundee, for funerary locations are another of my interests. As I walked back it began to drizzle, and having cleared during the morning the sky lowered itself to the rooftops, there to produce afresh the fog which made the

November afternoon of the smoke-fuelled earlier twentieth century so satisfyingly resemble the Victorian evening beloved of the painter Atkinson Grimshaw – also one of my subjects, I might add. On my return, the library was almost deserted.

As before, Quinn was malingering with a cigarette on the basement steps, directing at me a gaze of hopeless insolence. With a light heart I resumed my work.

When next I looked at my watch it was gone five o'clock. For a moment I could not think what had prompted me to break off from reading. Then it seemed to me that I remembered the sound of a page being turned – swiftly, impatiently turned. But there was no one else in the room. There never was. I listened. Nothing. Once more I bent my head to my task.

At six o'clock I heard St Nicholas's bells sounding for Evensong. And it seemed to me that just a moment before the bells began I had heard that abrupt sound again, of paper almost being torn, in impatience or haste. But the room still seemed full of its habitual centenarian silence. I worked on. At half past seven Quinn knocked on the door of the Silence Room. Time to lock up. I put what I needed in my briefcase, donned my overcoat and then, for no good reason I could discover, walked slowly down the aisles between the stacks, each in succession. All was as it should be in the autumn evening murk.

That night my concentration was poor. At ten I abandoned work and went to bed. But my re-reading of Gibbon held no charms. I lay awake for some time and after that my sleep was fitful. Normally my dreams are those of an administrator: in the city of dreams some small element of order needs to be restored; this accomplished, all shall be well. That night, however, I dreamed of a library. Not *the* library; though resembling it in many ways – the dome, the stairs to the basement, the caretaker's mop and bucket – but at the same time far larger, with archways leading to additional galleries, with spiral staircases ascending dizzyingly through the domes themselves, it seemed. It was silent and gas-lamps burned silently and there was a terrible atmosphere, an atmosphere of anticipation both dampened and sharpened, as if what was to happen could not happen until eternity had ended, but would certainly happen then. I had begun with disguised haste to make my way towards the exit when I woke up with a dry mouth. Until dawn I watched the clock and listened to the church bells across the city.

Quinn the caretaker's range of expression was not wide. It encompassed loathing, insubordination and a sense of unjust affliction. The next day as he shuffled to time from his cubby-hole near the washroom I could swear he looked at me with peculiar interest, like a man caught up in watching a horse-race. That morning it took an effort to enter the Silence Room and begin work; and before I began I once more patrolled the stacks.

You will not be surprised to hear that *A Hexhamshire Tragedy* had lost some of its power to compel. Since my Oxford days I had despised those – those many – who in a library cannot settle to their tasks but are endlessly up and down, distracted and distracting, even daring to seek the conversation of the occupied. Had I not been alone I might have done the same. But I struggled on until the lunch hour, when against my habit and inclination I went to the Tyneside Coffee Rooms, realizing as I sat over my spendthrift's bowl of soup (my sandwiches untouched in their greaseproof paper in my briefcase) that I was there in order to hear the voices of other people. I needed to float, if not to swim, in the warm tide of inane chatter with which all but the nth part of humanity occupies its unreflective leisure. In equal parts shame and terror I dragged my feet down Grey Street and Pudding Chare, back to the library, to the Silence Room. It seemed to be growing dusk already as I passed the raucous printers' bar near the newspaper office.

Work proceeded in a travesty of normality through the

afternoon. Nothing untoward occurred. At six o'clock I was tempted to finish early. I listened to St. Nicholas's bells and instructed myself to remain. The bells ceased. I looked down at my notes. Behind me a page turned.

I sprang up in terror to confront – to confront a spry white-haired man in an old-fashioned black suit, standing less than a yard away. He was aged perhaps seventy but in full health. His blue eyes regarded me brightly. A black bow tie and startlingly white shirt completed his attire. In his hands he held a slim black book the size of a volume of poems.

'Good evening,' he said, with a slight unplaceable accent. 'I take it I have the honour of meeting Leonard Dyas.'

'You have the advantage of me, sir,' I said, more calmly then I felt.

'My name is Reinhard Immerich, late of Nuremberg. Delighted to make your acquaintance at long last.'

'Why would you wish to do that?'

'That will require a little explanation. But now, my friend, I have found you. And you have found me.'

Summoning some self possession, I replied, 'I was not looking, Mr-'

'Doktor –'

'I wasn't looking, Doktor Immerich.'

'No? Who can say what we do in secret, in secret even from ourselves?'

'Are you a maker of riddles?' I asked, annoyance mixed with unease.

'Like yourself, I aspired to be a maker of sense.'

'I do not think you are a member here. How did you gain entry?'

'I am a reader like you. Libraries are my home.'

'Nevertheless –'

'Nevertheless,' – he put a white hand on my arm, his eyes brightening and seeming to dilate a little – 'nevertheless there are matters of mutual concern requiring urgent attention.' He saw my doubt and anger and said, 'I shall explain, in the proper order. We have a little time. Please, sit.'

To be honest, I needed to sit. My strange companion remained standing close at hand, attentive as a waiter or an executioner. He might have been older than seventy, I thought, but he was wiry and vigorous. As he gazed unblinkingly at me, I felt a migraine about to begin. Soon the first tiny interference, the first spectra, would appear minutely in the corner of my eye, growing from there to consume the whole of my consciousness in a roar of pain.

'This book,' he said, ' is what you have been searching for.'

'I beg your pardon?'

'Take it.'

'But what is it called?'

'Ah, if we knew that.' He placed a white hand on my arm. The spectra swarmed across his face. I looked down. They swarmed across the floor.

'Is this a game?' I asked, struggling to keep my eyes open. Nausea would follow. I needed to lie down.

'You do not want the book? Very well.' He grimaced sadly and made to turn away.

'Wait. I don't understand.'

'Then take the book.' He held it out again.

I must have lost a second or two. Now the book was in my hands, slightly heavy for its size. I turned it over and made to open it, though in my condition heaven knows what I expected to see inside it.

'Not here,' he said, laying the white hand on the cover. 'Save it for the privacy of your apartment.'

'There are questions – ' I began.

Quinn knocked heavily on the door.

'And now you must leave,' said Immerich. He helped me up and guided me towards the door.

'What about you?' I said.

Then I was standing outside, blinking as the migraine diminished. Quinn stood waiting. If he had heard me talking he gave no indication.

'Last as usual, Mr Dyas,' he said.

'Of course, Quinn. If I were not, the world would fall from its orbit.'

He smirked, rattled his keys – as if *he* owned the place – and gestured me up the stairs. Of Immerich there was no sign.

At home I placed the book on my desk and then made myself prepare supper and eat it while listening to the news on the wireless. Not until I had washed up did I allow myself back into the study, where I examined the book under a powerful lamp without as yet opening it. The book was, as I thought, oddly heavy. It was odourless and its black binding was hide of some sort I could not identify. I noted these points in my journal and then at length opened the book. On the title page was printed in plain black type **The Book**. There was no author's name nor publishing details nor date on the verso. Beyond that there was nothing at all but a bank of creamy blank pages – in which it was very tempting to begin to write, if one could have mustered anything memorable to say. I closed the book and set it aside again. It lay on the edge of the lamplight, reflecting nothing and admitting less. This was clearly a practical joke of an especially elaborate kind. Quinn was the obvious candidate, though the sophistication of the game made him a doubtful conspirator. I was forced to admire the trick, even as I decided to get to the bottom of the matter.

Then I opened the book again and turned past the title page, noticing as I did so that the act of turning the pages, though I performed it delicately, produced a disproportionately loud sound, like tearing. Before I could consider this, print appeared on the page before me. I blinked; this might be an effect of the now-vanished migraine. But the print remained on the page, and as I began to read I knew with a sudden punch to the heart that before me lay a poem, by Baudelaire, a sonnet: moreover, I knew with exultant certainty that I was the first, the only person,

146

other than the author, ever to have read it. Without letting go of the book I reached across the desk for a sheet of paper and a pencil in order to copy out the text. But when I looked back the sonnet was disappearing line by line, from the bottom upwards. When I turned over the next page was blank. When I turned back, so was the first. I dropped the book. It closed, gently.

I felt forcibly that here was something unnatural and vile. I resisted the urge to fling the book across the room or into the fire, or to wash my hands. I poured a drink, went to the mantelpiece and examined the book from afar in the mirror. Nothing happened, of course. When I went back to the desk I found I could not remember a single word of the poem. Not that I supposed it to exist, as I intended to prove by further examination of the book.

I opened it again at random. The page was blank. But then there was another poem, this time indisputably by W.B. Yeats, late work known only to me, the black type testifying that it had always been there, though I knew that I alone had seen it. Once more I made to copy the poem; once more the words wriggled their way intolerably down the page, out of the world and out of my memory. Though shaken, I resolved on a third and final attempt. Again the blank appeared, and then, again, in a moment or two the immortal type – but this time…this time the poem was mine, the great lyric was mine, whispering its musical secret to the desert air!

And if it was mine, how could I lose? Goodbye to *A Hexhamshire Tragedy* and all the other dryasdust trash of the ages: the world lay all before the poet Dyas! I took up the pencil. Once more the words began to slip away. I cried out in pain. The very act of trying to record the words seemed to accelerate their departure. All gone. If this was my poem, though, then I would remember. But I did not remember – not a line, not a word, not a letter, not the shape of the incomparable rhythms sketched on the inner ear. All I could remember was the fact of forgetting. It was as if I had died.

As I sat there my migraine came again and blinded me.

I must have undressed in a trance, since I found myself in bed when I woke to crisp winter sunlight. Even as the year dies, the city is at its most heartening on such a day: frost in the lungs holds out the promise of immortality.

Quinn greeted me sullenly as he unlocked the street entrance and as I passed through the main library the issue desk was still dark. I switched on the lights to the basement stairs and went down. At the bottom I reached out towards the door of the Silence Room, then paused to look round at the dingy hallway and its third-rate paintings before going in. I could hear a tap – still unrepaired – running in the washroom. I opened the door.

'You are mercifully prompt,' said Immerich, attired as before in black, though seeming a little anxious and weary.

'Take your book,' I said, thrusting it at him.

'You will need it, my friend' he said, with his little bright-eyed smile. 'As you will discover. There is little time. Take my arm, please.' He led me into a far a corner of the room. My confusion was compounded by the sight of a wrought-iron spiral staircase going down through the floor.

'But this – does not exist,' I said.

'You must go first,' said Immerich, placing that vile white hand on my arm. My will, it seemed, was not my own; or it worked secretly. You must decide. We descended perhaps two dozen steps in a shaft in the black dark, Immerich's hand now on my shoulder. At the foot of the steps stood a door, leather-covered, slightly ajar.

'Enter,' breathed Immerich. I pushed the door open.

I saw, impossibly, the library. Yet I did not, as a second glance revealed. It was the library magnified – the central gold-blue dome dizzyingly far aloft, the atrium countless storeys high, through which spiral staircases swarmed spiderlike as though in the moment of a dreadful mechanical genesis. Sconces burned on the vast pillars. Arches led off in every direction to further hinted galleries which I knew

148

would be as vast as this, each with its array of further exits. Everything I needed was here.

'Exactly,' said Immerich.

I turned to face him. The door through which we had come had vanished. A thrill of panic ran up my spine and into my brain.

'What is this place?'

'This is the library, of course,' he replied. A wave of pain, then a wave of relief, passed over his face. 'This is what you have been looking for always.'

'I have?'

'Soon you will know it, Mr Dyas.'

'But how do I get out?'

'That is the question,' he said. 'It depends on you. Can you return to the world? Or not? There is no one to find you. Can you open the door again? Or do you seek immortal solitude among these empty halls?' Once again my head flooded with terror; once again my migraine hinted itself. I looked at Immerich as the spectra swam over his face and the shelves behind him. There was a great question I could ask, if only I could frame it. My tongue was thick in my mouth. As I struggled I saw Immerich beginning as it were to fade, his jacket-cuffs fraying into dust, his hands shrinking, his white, bright-eyed face seeming to fold in on itself and the shelves appearing flickeringly through his ragged outline. 'Ah, my friend,' he said, in a rusty croak, 'it is true what *The Book of Ecclesiastes* says: 'Vanity, all is vanity. Of the making of many books there is no end.'' And he was gone, a swirl of dust-motes that glittered in the absent sun.

I awoke in a chair at a nearby desk, awoke to the prospect of eternal solitude, of terror with neither object nor cause, save for the intolerable fact of consciousness itself. The horror of this place was its perfection – and its perfect silence. For days I wandered without hunger or thirst, browsing the texts of my doom. What did I discover? That in the library there was nothing left to aspire to. There was no work so grand, no iconoclasm so startling, no tradition so secure, no ingenuity so trivial that it was not already somewhere to be found in this, the immutable and unreadable temple of perfection – the imaginary museum made over into print and paper.

Even desperation has it habits. To read was a sort of distraction, though without sleep my reading and notemaking soon turned into a delirium of precision, out of which the name of a project soon – in fifty years, you say? – whispered itself to me like evil. Should I read wisely, then perhaps I could discover – you are ahead of me perhaps – my successor, yes, the next true resident of these accursed galleries and catalogues. It is too late, my friend. Too late to leave, too late now to regain the fallen vulgar world. You took the book and read in it. And see, the door by which we entered is now vanished. All that remains for me is to vanish too, released into blessed extinction, and for you to set about your work, custodian of this, the greatest library of all. Farewell, Custodian, farewell.

Three Fevers

You find them near the exit doors of libraries. This is a case in point: an oilcloth-covered table with an apologetic scattering of unwanted books seeking places in which to end their days, though in all likelihood their days are already done. This is where we all go, eventually, you might think, whether writers or not – into the void of disregard, beneath time's indifferent gaze (though at some point even the clock overhead will be unceremoniously taken down and dumped in a skip, with its innards hanging out like a cartoon). All those lives' works, remaindered and worse than remaindered, here. The novels that seemed most likely to last; the unreadable thrillers of a decade ago; the groundbreaking studies; the touching / exciting / remarkable / refreshing debuts. This idle paragraph too is subject to the law: in which case better print it somewhere first, give it the ghost of a half-life at least.

*

Three Fevers. Leo Walmlsey. Red Penguin. Price – . Published -. Rusty with salt. On the windowsill of the holiday house in 197-. Along with Ngaio Marsh and Josephine Tey, with *Rogue Male*, *Casino Royale*, *Precious Bane*, *Frenchman's Creek* and *Cautionary Verses*, *Reader's Digest* and *Lilliput*.

The damp in the hallway has waited all winter to greet you. The morning is overcast and as you near the coast the cloud comes down and turns to sea-roke, so the place is hard to find, one of innumerable turnings off the boggy tops.

*

The drunk at seven o'clock is baffled by your lack of interest. He appeals to your better instincts. His life is what he is trying to convey, first to you and then to your female companion. She plays against contemporary expectations by seeming to require you to do something about this melancholy intruder you want to see the back of but feel guilty about because it *is his life* he is trying to communicate to you with these expansive gestures. His consciousness is by now so edited down that it's all peaks and troughs, exuberance pushed aside by despair, sudden enlightenment having the door slammed in its face by the knowledge that he's been here before in a hundred incarnations, trying and failing simultaneously to raid the inarticulate and hold the attention of the passing trade.

'Is she your lass?' You say nothing. 'Is she your lass? Is she? I'm just asking a question pal, all right. Is – she – your – lass?' Actually, you don't know whether she is or not, or whether either of you wants her to be, because it's too early to tell. You have to say something. You are sitting too close to the open fire and you want to move, but the drunk is leaning in, swaying, affectionate, tearful, on the brink of fury.

Eventually the woman says, 'Look, we're just having a quiet drink. Leave us alone, OK?

'OK?' the drunk says, significantly, as if his suspicions have been confirmed. With a conspiratorial smile, he nods and looks round for the support of the imaginary companions he meets most evenings around this time. 'OK? Hear that? She's OK. Right y'are, pet. Hey pal – ' he jabs you in the arm with his forefinger – 'you wanna look after her, she's a pearl beyond price, a pearl beyond fookin price. A soft voice is a wonderful thing in a woman, although – paradosically – ' Two barmen have come up quietly alongside him now, their hands extended as though to receive a pass from a loose scrum. 'On the other hand she is more bitter than death, yeah?'

'Right, Derek,' says one of the barmen quietly, 'let's be having you now. Let's not have any bother.'

'No bother,' says the drunk, affably. 'No bother. Nae fookin bother. Sorry pet.' They drag him away.

*

You pick up the copy of *Three Fevers*. The idea is to contribute something, a few coppers, to the library. It's very simple. Put twenty pence in the tin, put the book in your pocket, move on to the next thing. For the moment you can't remember what the next thing is meant to be.

You look at the clock and remember, with a pang of something that could be guilt, or duty, or desire.

*

She's late. You explore the house a bit, unable to settle. You put the kettle on and notice the holiday smell of gas. The roke stands at the kitchen window, parting a little sometimes to show the sundial on the sodden lawn. It's too early for this. It's too cold for the seaside. You check the radiators. As promised, they're on to warm the place through. The bed feels a bit damp, though. You light the fire laid in the grate. You leaf through the books on the windowsill. Some you've read, some you never will. *Three Fevers* falls into neither category. You go and turn down the counterpane, with a faint sense of disquiet, as if you're presuming. But isn't that why you're here, or part of it anyway? A long way to come otherwise, you think, as you make a cup of tea you don't want, and the dim afternoon tilts towards evening. You leave a note and walk down the hill to the beach. Soon she will be here. This is just the before part.

There is no beach, really. At low tide there are wide plates of rock stretching away under the fog. The place feels like a building site or something damaged, smeared with malevolent black-green weed. You walk gingerly out, far enough to lose sight of the shore, then stop. Waves break in the distance. The whole place, the huge stone socket of the bay, the wintry village with its rags of bunting strung between the two pubs, seems to be waiting. You go on another twelve steps until you see a skin of water rising over a lip of rock.

You go back to the house. Her car is not outside. You think of ringing but that could be awkward and anyway she will be travelling. That is to say, she will already have left. You pick up the copy of *Three Fevers* and walk down to the Ship. In the bar a couple of locals sit in the yellow silence with pints of mild. The lounge is freezing but you want to be on your own. The landlady puts a light on for you.

You take out the book and read the biographical note about the author, then put the book back in your pocket. Seven o'clock. Hard to say whether this amounts to lateness or not. What were you expecting?

You read the local paper from cover to cover and now it is half past seven. You order another pint and some peanuts. The house is nearly visible from the window of the lounge.

*

You put twenty pence in the tin and turn the book over in your hands. You read the biographical note. Leo Walmsley was a famous novelist in his time, up there with Howard Spring and Warwick Deeping, but gone now, it seems, as irrevocably as silent film. That was the impression of him you got in the holiday house, in the village. He was a local author there. He was a real presence, like the Grand National or the Boat Race, fundamental, like Captain Webb on a matchbox, like dense mattresses of ambient smoke in documentary films about the North – something unquestionably *there*, as England was *there*; and as she was not. You do not bring her name to mind. You do not need to. Instead you think of 'The Work of Art in the Era of Mechanical Reproduction.' And you remember having sex in the lee of a wall behind the palm house, suddenly finding yourselves doing it, a bit pissed, amused rather than scared at the idea of being caught. But desperately urgent, as if something was at stake. The heels of her sandals dug into the backs of your knees. It was a muggy night with shreds of fog under the trees in the park. You had a copy of MacNeice's poems in your jacket pocket. It kept banging against you, so you removed it and placed it on a brick. She took the opportunity to put her pants in her shoulderbag before you continued. The night was holding its hot, damp breath as if something was about to happen. With all the chestnut trees it was like being in a candelabra'd ballroom after the event, when the coaches had taken the guests away and the servants could indulge themselves among the leftovers.

You put the copy of *Three Fevers* in your pocket and go to keep your evening's appointment.

*

In the pub you realize your companion has been watching you for some time.

'Sorry, Jan,' you say. 'Something just reminded me. You know.'

'What of?' She smiles sympathetically.

'I don't know.'

'Shall we get off, then?' She is already on her feet.

There is a jazz event you are meant to be going to. You like jazz. You don't mind sitting with the other ageing aficionados in grubby pub concert rooms with only one sort of lager on and no Guinness, even though there are hardly any women in this world. Tonight, though, you feel absolutely exhausted. But it would be death (the death of what?) to pull out now. It's much too late for that kind of complication. You go slowly down towards the quayside, passing the Lit and Phil library where the book manifested itself to you. You wonder if you should mention this, but what exactly is there to mention? You navigate like a sensible, tolerant, grown-up couple past the bellowing herds of stags and the screeching flocks of hens, and all the time you wonder if it's too late to be here now, starting something you perhaps can't finish. What must your companion be thinking? She has, as they say, made an effort.

'I like the way you've had your hair done,' you say. 'And your jacket. Is that new?' She nods. Now it is her turn to be elsewhere.

'Shall we have another drink first?' she asks, stepping off the pavement and into the Crown Posada without waiting for a reply. It is one of the quiet intervals of the evening – unpredictable half hours when you can get a seat before the human wave breaks back up the hill. She leaves you to order and finds a table down at the far end. The choice of position seems ominous. By the hatch, as ever, stands the solitary silver-haired man with the hare lip, drinking one of the dozen pints he soberly gets through on the average night. It is hard to imagine that he has ever had sex. The same could be said of you and your companion. You haven't, of course, not with each other. You think the two of you must look resigned to an awkward accommodation, like bitter pensioners eating their ice creams in an empty matinee cinema while those on screen grind away obliviously. You've seen lots of couples like yourselves in this pub – sort-of couples, maybe couples, clandestine couples, former couples, uneasy pairings just about functioning by means of varying ratios of goodwill and need, like people brought together by rail crashes or wartime bombing, long after the cruel, exciting glamour of the accident has worn away, when the ordinariness stretches ahead for the rest of your lifetimes without parole. It is a good thing the mirrors on the opposite wall are placed too high for you to see yourselves. You wish you had something to read, apart from *Three Fevers*, which you have not even begun and never will. You know that down in the snug there is a shelf of books, car manuals mainly. You wonder who would spend an evening reading a car manual. Or 'consulting' one. You have not consulted memory: it has simply moved in and occupied the space where once you were.

'Right, what is it?' she says when you sit down with the drinks. You have somehow bought yourself a large vodka as well as a pint.

Your hand has gone to your pocket.

'What have you got there?'

'Sorry?'

'You keep fingering it. What is it?'

'A book.'

'Let's see.'

You hand it to her.

'Never heard of him. Why've you bought this? It's ancient.' She is quizzical but still theoretically friendly. Her comments are probably fatal, though. Is she in fact talking about the book? You drink half your pint in a single swallow.

'Steady,' she says. 'Look. What's wrong?'

*

You could not swear how many pints you've had. At half past nine you rise carefully and leave the still-empty pub, giving the landlady a stately nod which clearly doesn't fool her at all. You go back up the hill, a little breathless and sidelong in the cold. The roke has finally cleared, now that there is nothing to see. The house is dark. The only car is yours. You go into the kitchen, switch on the light and come out again. You bring *Three Fevers* with you and place it on the grass by the sundial's base. In the faint light from the kitchen you struggle to read the inscription around the clockface of the sundial. *My days are as a shadow that declineth.*

'Amen to that,' you announce to the night in general and set off back downhill to use the phone in the pub. When you ask the landlady for change you find yourself explaining that your friend is late, but clearly she would rather you didn't go into it. Your distress must be evident. You order a large Bell's and stand it in the top of the telephone coinbox.

The phone is answered immediately.

'Now then, now then, who's this?' The speaker is clearly drunk. He sounds as if he has been waiting for this moment. A hand brushes over the mouthpiece but you hear a woman laughing in the background, then several voices, all it up with drink. They're all there, all of them.

'Is Karen there, please?'

More laughter. Muffled exchanges. The receiver put down heavily.

Then someone picks it up.

'Yes?'

'Karen?

'What do you want?' She sounds irritated.

'I'm here. Where the fuck are you?'

'Where the fuck am I? I should have thought that was obvious.' More laughter. The phone is put down.

Back at the house you manage to light a fire in the kitchen grate. You go out and retrieve *Three Fevers* from the lawn, then kneel by the fire, tear the book up and feed it a few pages at a time into the flames. Even though you're drunk you can sense that this is not really adequate (never mind necessary) in symbolic terms, but that it is also irrevocable. Something has been done forever. You go to sleep on the settee in the garden lounge in the house that comfortably sleeps six.

*

When you get sober you go home and read a lot of books, about twenty years' worth at an average of four a week, and you become approximately as well read as you hoped to be.

You never read *Three Fevers* or anything else by Leo Walmsley, though you never forget a name. Once there is an item about him on the regional television news. Someone is attempting to open a museum dedicated to him in the village. This sounds at once understandable and slightly mad, as though everyone should have a museum opened in their names. How could there be enough memoriousness to go round? You and she might have to take on the task of each other's museums. What would you put in hers? A pub telephone, a couple of hotel rooms, a long silence interrupted by laughter on some topic you're not privy to.

You read a good deal of poetry. You must be reading the rations meant for others. You encounter a poem by Douglas Dunn, which imagines a couple waltzing in foggy meadows near the edge of cliffs. You find that without intending to you have committed it to memory. Whenever the poem surfaces, you flinch a little.

*

'Because you do seem very bothered this evening,' your companion says. 'Is it me? Have I done something? Do you want me to go?'

'No,' you say. She stands up. 'Hang on.' She sits down again, perching on the edge of the bench, her jacket and bag still in her folded arms.

'Well?'

You are very tired. You have never been so tired in your life. She looks at her watch and bites her tongue.

'It's about this poem.'

'What, one in that book?'

'No.'

'What poem, then?'

'You know that drunk?'

'What about him.'

'It's like that.'

'What is? Like what? What on earth are you on about?'
'I dunno.'
'Well then.' She stands up again. 'Let's leave it, eh?'

You have no comment to make on this. She leaves. She actually walks out without looking back. You search for your feelings about this, but now you are inert as a sodden log in a canal. No one should aim any expectations your way for a bit. You stock up on vodka, which you never drink normally, and you sit while the pub fills and empties. Anyone looking might see you flinch as the poem rises into your mind again: 'Your hand, and my hand, and your face that I cannot see.'

Kiss Me Deadly
on the Museum Island

I would be prepared to bet a large sum that the works of Mickey Spillane are not represented in the library. Mike Hammer? Mr Hardboiled himself. *Of course*, you might say, *his day is gone. History found him insufficiently interesting.* History? You mean librarians. *Or insufficiently hardboiled. You should read some of the stuff they get in nowadays: enough to make your pubes stand on end.* If you say so.

I was about to explain my own involvement in the works of the creator of Mike Hammer. And I discover to my alarm that the episode in question took place fifteen years ago, in 1989. I was a young man, recently appointed in the Department, immersed in my studies, eager for anywhere they might take me. A man of the Left, also, as they say in Europe. A sentimentalist, as we say nowadays; but I have never understood that word completely.

My subject was the brothers Mann, Heinrich and Thomas – the socialist and the nationalist, the satirist and the elegist, the victim and the survivor, the implacably twinned authors of *Mephisto* and *Doktor Faustus*. What was my subject, really? I think it was probably the idea of my own seriousness against a historical backdrop of vast terror and exhilaration. Anyway. That April I was due to take part – in my other persona, which it may surprise you to hear was that of poet – in a translation seminar. This was held at a conference centre in Glienicke, in West Berlin, near the famous Bridge of

161

Spies. Things seemed to slot pleasingly into place. Inbound for Tegel, the plane seemed to me to descend on the very core of Europe. There it lay in the green spring chill, the sandy lakes and the Grünwald and all those loaded names – Potsdam, Spandau, Wannsee, and the political island of the city itself. Speaking objectively, who could resist? Has anyone ever managed to do so? Who could resist the way the Wall itself ran through the middle of the outbuildings of this old hunting lodge? Who would not be beguiled by the bucolic menace of a Vopo patrol boat nosing along through the Death Zone of the lake?

Then I fell in love, there by the lake in the woods where signs – You Are Now Leaving the American Zone – stand knee-deep in the water: and where at dawn you may hear the melodic hysteria of the nightingales. Steffi was a translator, a freelance brought in through the offices of one of the cultural organizations lending its support to the conference. She had the sallow, slightly sluttish good looks you find among dark-haired German girls, along with a harsh smoker's laugh and an intense professional seriousness about Rilke and Holderlin and Brecht that was just as arousing as the legs she wrapped around me when the nightingales began their blue jazz.

We never missed a seminar all week. I don't remember sleeping; nor do I remember how the affair got under way. I remember her room – books, papers, overflowing ashtrays, scattered underwear, and her critical but encouraging gaze from beneath her fringe as she sat astride me, urging me to redouble my efforts. She would come with a harsh groan, lie back for a minute, then light her umpteenth cigarette.

'I'll end up smoking if I stay with you,' I told her once.

'That's good. I'm looking for converts.'

'Do you have a preferred brand? *Roth Händles?*'

'Na. I smoke anything. The point is to smoke, to be engaged in smoking. You should have a shower.'

'Really?'

162

'You stink.'

'Then I stink of you.'

'It's a labour of love,' she said, then closed her eyes against the smoke.

On the last evening of the conference we absconded from the regimented dining room to a place in the woods – beer and sausage for political tourists in the chilly lanterned arbour where we talked as a prelude to further bouts of helpless fucking. Steffi was from the East. Her parents got out just before Ulbricht sealed the border. She had never seen her grandparents or aunts or uncles, all still living in Leipzig. She was a woman of the Left, she said; Maoist, not Stalinist, of course.

'The distinction's academic, isn't it? Really' I said. She gave me one of her looks. 'I mean, I sympathise, of course, but given the location, the present tendency of history and so on -'

'Fuck you, Richard,' she said equably. 'History? History has nothing to do with you. You're a tourist, remember. Worse, you're English. Finish your dinner.'

I was drunk and could not keep my mouth shut.

'What will we do now that it's over – the conference?'

She shrugged and blew smoke in my face.

'You will go back, I suppose.'

'Not necessarily.'

'You should not overrate this experience. Yes, I am as you say a lovely fuck. But I am not England.'

'I don't want England.'

'You will.'

'I'll be the judge of that.'

She smiled and reached for my hand.

'All the women in my family tell fortunes as well as being Marxists. This line – ' she squeezed my palm roughly, like a masseuse – 'is for love. And this –' again, harder – 'is for brains.'

'And what do you conclude?'

'That if your brains were as big as your cock you would be another Hegel.'

'Well, that's something.'

She gathered her things together and stood up.

'Let's go tonight,' she said.

'What? And miss the final plenary?'

'Regrettably, yes.'

'Where shall we go?'

'I'll take you to my place.'

I had not thought of Steffi as having a *place*. I suppose I thought she simply manifested herself in a professional context from time to time and inbetweenwhiles vanished. I began to explain this.

'Well, let's find out,' she said. That was her Trabant in the car park. As we drove through the dark she pointed out of the window and said. 'That's where they did it.'

'What is?'

'Wannsee. The Wannsee Conference.' Somehow ashamed, I stared into the dark and saw nothing. 'That is why Comrade Ulbricht punished everyone. It was for our own good.' She laughed.

Steffi lived in Kreuzberg, near Gropiusstadt, in a street of Turkish grocers and cafes, in a tall, ancient-looking block with no lights in the lobby. The lift was antique and very slow. She put her head against my chest and we rose slowly through the creaking dark, through smells of cooking and sounds of radio music and other people's domesticity.

'This is as far as we go,' she said, leading me across a corridor under a faintly orange skylight. Music came through the door of the apartment. She unlocked the door and called, 'Irmgard, is that you?'

I had not expected Irmgard. Irmgard might be an impediment to the urgent final intimacy I think I was seeking. There was no reply. A door at the end of the hall opened on to a large room. The far wall taken up by a window, beyond which lay a balcony. The glass door to the balcony was open.

We went out. Steps led down to a roof area with, unexpectedly, a pool, in which a woman was swimming laps. She saw us, stopped and took off her pink goggles. We approached.

'Richard, this is Irmgard. She is a lesbian.'

'Excellent,' I said, reminding myself of William Whitelaw.

'Richard is a poet.'

'Well –' I began.

'Another one?' said Irmgard, climbing effortlessly from the pool to stand streaming on the tiles. 'I thought you were finished with them,'

'Richard is different,' said Steffi, laughing. She handed Irmgard a towel.

'As you wish, Liebchen,' said Irmgard. 'Would you excuse me, Richard?' Irmgard towelled her blonde hair fiercely and went indoors.

'I feel I'm intruding,' I said.

'Don't worry about Irmgard. She feels protective towards me. It is her way.'

'And do you need her to protect you?'

'Let's have a drink.'

We sat on the settee drinking beer. The evening seemed to be running out of steam. I wondered if I should have come. Irmgard reappeared in street clothes. She smiled awkwardly, then looked expectantly at Steffi.

'Well?'

'Not yet. We have only just arrived.'

'You must try,' said Irmgard. 'I must go to work.'

'What do you do?'

'I work in a nightclub,' she said.

When Irmgard had gone I asked, 'What kind of nightclub?'

'Not the sort you imagine.'

'Pardon me.'

'Not like some filthy Kirchner painting. It is a comedy club. A club of satirists and small plays of the Left, even

165

sometimes of poets. Irmgard says she works there. In fact she owns it. This flat is hers. I am her tenant. Are you disappointed?' Steffi smiled and laughed her racking laugh.

'Should I have come here, though? I mean really.'

'Let me show you.'

As it began to grow light there was no sign of Irmgard. I had promised myself a trip through Checkpoint Charlie, but with Steffi that was not an option.

'Have you been across the wall? You must have,' Steffi said.

'No. I was planning to.'

'Today? Then you must go.'

'But what about you?'

She smiled.

'I have work, Richard. I am not so economically autonomous that I can spend all my time fucking, not even with you.'

'I don't want to waste time I could spend with you.'

'Why? Is this a holiday romance?'

'I hope not.'

'I will be here when you return. After that we shall see.'

'If you're sure.'

'Go to East Berlin, Richard. Walk around. It may not be there forever.'

'That's not what I've heard.'

'You could do me a favour.'

'Of course.'

'I need you to take something through with you.'

'I'm sorry?'

'It's a small thing only.'

'Wouldn't that be dangerous?'

'Hardly. No matter. Forget it.' She smiled and went through into the kitchen. I followed. She filled the coffee pot and stared out of the window.

'I'm sorry,' I said. 'You caught me —'

'Off guard. So I see.' Again the unbearably sweet smile

that said: *You're only human. Like the others. Like those other poets here before you.*

'I suppose I am worried in case it's dangerous,' I said. She shrugged, smiled again and busied herself with cups. 'Is it dangerous?'

'What can I tell you, Richard? There is a tiny risk, yes. I should not have asked. We will forget it.'

Oh, no, we won't. This failure of yours will be our definition, you coward.

'What is it you want me to carry through?'

'It no longer matters.' She handed me a cup and went into the living room.

'Just tell me,' I said, my embarrassment crossing over into anger. Tried and found wanting.

She studied me as she lit a cigarette.

'Sure?'

I nodded.

'It is a book.'

'What kind of book?'

'A small one.'

'I mean, what is it about?'

'I have not read it.'

'For fuck's sake, Steffi.'

'So. Our first argument.'

'Can I see it?' She went to the shelves and came back with a small paperback. 'Let me see.'

It was a 1952 first edition paperback of *Kiss Me Deadly*.

'Is this a joke?'

She shrugged.

'Is it?' I repeated.

'To you perhaps.'

'This is a pulp crime novel. It's hardly – I dunno – Hayek or Friedman, is it?'

'*De gustibus*' said Steffi.

'I'm not sure the censors would agree with you there. Anyway, have you read it?'

'It is not for me.'

'Of course. Then who is it for?'

'My uncle.'

I saw the uncle sitting in his vest at his tower block kitchen table, longing for the garbage of the Fascist West.

'Fuck. Why this?'

'Ask him.'

'Perhaps I will. I mean, this isn't even really pornography.'

'Have you read it?'

'No.'

'Then how can you tell what it is?'

'I just know.'

'How convenient.' She opened the window and let in a blast of chill air.' So are you refusing because you are frightened, or on the grounds of taste?'

'I didn't say I was refusing.'

'Are you sure?'

'Why does your uncle want this book?'

'That's not your concern.'

'It is if I have to carry the book across the border.'

'"The border!" Whoooo! "The border!"' She waved her arms in a ghostly way. 'Quick, everyone! Run before the giant crabs devour us!'

'Now you're being silly.'

'What is it? You want me to suck your cock? OK.'

'No – I mean, yes, but not for that reason.'

'You are a confused boy, Richard.'

'Why does your uncle – supposing he is your bloody uncle – want this crappy book?'

She looked at me from under her fringe.

'Because in addition to being a professor of history he likes pulp crime novels. Hank Janson, Peter Cheyney, James Hadley Chase. And Mickey Spillane above all. Don't ask me why. Why did Stalin like Chaplin?'

'That's not the same.'

'So will you take it for me?'

'That's all. No funny business?'

'Who am I, Richard?'

'We've scarcely been introduced, darling.'

'Yes, but what am I? Olga Bendova the beautiful spy, fucking my way to the final triumph of capitalism and/or Actually Existing Socialism? Is that what you think?'

'Of course not.'

'Well, then, Richard, the conclusion seems evident. Either you are a coward, or you take a teeny-tiny little risk. You think they waste time searching tourists?'

We parted at the front door. We would rendezvous at the flat in the evening.

Checkpoint Charlie? Checkpoint Charlie was simply an indoor queue. The hare-eyed young guards wasted no time on me.

Released into the wide, empty streets of Mitte I tried to summon appropriate feelings. The corner of a huge nineteenth century block – warehousing, offices, nothing at all but partitioned shadows? – was pocked with bullet holes. It looked like a grey cheese. Posters on chained gateways showed the Party lists for the forthcoming elections. Greedy for more actuality I wandered a little way north and found a workmen's café where I ate a piece of rubbery torte, watched neutrally by two middle-aged waitresses from the curtained kitchen doorway.

This indulgence meant I had to rush to meet Professor Gisevius. But I was the first one to arrive among the sooty domes of the Museum Island. The air was thick with the smell of coal. Though the day was chilly I was sweating into my shirt. I leaned on the parapet and looked into the grey river's waters. So far there was nothing wrong, was there? I was a tourist, taking in the major landmarks. At any moment I could go home if I chose. I could throw the damn book in the river.

'Herr Doktor Richard Joyce?'

Professor Gisevius had come up silently, like a barge on the dark water. He tilted his head with a questioning smile, a fit looking man of sixty-odd with thick white hair and silver-rimmed spectacles. He wore a heavy black coat.

'Professor Gisevius.'

'Good. Let us go. It is cold today, I think.'

'Where shall we go?'

'There is an office. There we can talk and take refreshments.'

'I don't want to be too long.'

'Naturally.' He gestured ahead. A black Wartburg drew up at the kerb and the driver got out. A solid, fair young man, dressed like a student, he held open the door.

'Please,' said Gisevius.

'You have a chauffeur?'

'Are you my chauffeur, Reiner?' Gisevius called.

Reiner smiled widely and said nothing. Gisevius and I climbed into the back of the car and we drove off.

'Where is the office?'

'It is not far. How is my niece?'

'She is well. She sends her love.'

'Of course.'

'Have you any message for her?'

Gisevius turned and smiled. Reiner laughed.

'Tell her – tell her to be good,' said Gisevius. Reiner was beside himself. We turned with a jolt. in though an archway and into a small courtyard. The windows on the ground floor were blacked out. Reiner climbed out and closed the gate. I saw him swing a bunch of keys before returning them to his pocket.

'Where are we?' I asked.

'Here is the office,' said Gisevius. Reiner opened the door and gestured me out. There were six stories of blackened brick and blacked out windows. The sky seemed a long way off and full of snow.

We went through a goods entrance with rubber doors and into a freight lift.

'This isn't the university, is it?' I asked.

Reiner slammed the safety gate shut. Gisevius looked at me with a tolerant smile.

'We must work with what we have,' he said.

We stopped at the top floor. Reiner opened the gate and ushered me into the dim corridor.

'What is going to happen?' I asked.

'Capitalism will in time fail,' said Gisevius. Reiner brought up the rear.

'I mean – '

'My office,' said Gisevius, indicated a glass-panelled door lit from within. The painted lettering on the glass read *Oskar Gisevius: Privatdetektiv.* 'After you, Herr Doktor.' I turned and looked at Reiner, who shrugged good-humouredly and glanced back towards the lift before shaking his head. 'Please. Time is not long.'

The outer office, its windows black, lit by a desk-lamp, contained a hatstand, a desk, a filing cabinet and an office chair in which Steffi sat filing her nails. She wore a suit from forty years before. Another upright chair faced the desk.

'Steffi.'

'Did you bring the book, Richard?'

'What are you doing here?'

'Take Doktor Joyce's coat, Reiner,' said Gisevius.

Reiner helped me out of my coat, hung it on the hatstand, then pressed me down into the chair.

'Did you bring the book, Richard?' Steffi asked again.

'I don't understand what's happening.'

Gisevius nodded. Reiner opened the filing cabinet and took out a metal toolbox. He placed it on the desk and opened it.

Gisevius looked in the box and thought for a while. Then he pointed.

'That one.'

Reiner produced a pair of pliers.

'Jesus,' I said.

'The book, Richard,' said Steffi.

'What? It's in my coat pocket. Is this about the book?'

'What else?' asked Gisevius. 'Is there something else?'

'What? No. I mean, I brought the book as requested. As instructed.'

Reiner handed *Kiss Me Deadly* to the Professor. He opened it and sniffed the gutter exultantly.

'Beautiful. You should smell this, Reiner. Original Signet edition. Woodpulp. 'Quality Reading for the Millions', yes? Reiner modestly declined. Steffi wrinkled her nose with distaste.

'So are you finished with the pliers?' I asked.

'Not quite,' said Gisevius, sitting on the edge of the desk. He leaned forward and handed me the book.

'What do you want me to do?'

'Surely that is obvious, Doktor Joyce.' He sat back and folded his arms. Steffi lit a cigarette and stared haughtily at the blacked-out window. Reiner lay on his back, propping his head on his hands.

*

'Enough,' said Professor Gisevius after an hour. He took the book from me and placed it in his pocket. 'You read very well. What do you think, Steffi?' She made a little moue of boredom and produced a powder compact. 'Reiner?'

'Mike Hammer is a revolver,' said Reiner.

'You mean a pistol,' Steffi snapped.

'Entschuldigen,' said Reiner.

'More to the point,' said Gisevius, 'he delivers an immanent critique of the system he purports to sustain. Am I correct?' He looked at me.

'Possibly. I haven't read the whole book.'

'Shame on you.'

'I like the girls also,' said Reiner.

'You mean you like the confusion of sex and violence. You are an animal,' said Steffi without looking at him.

'We are all animals,' said Reiner good-naturedly.

'Speak for yourself,' said Steffi.

'Can I go now?' I asked.

'Possibly,' said Gisevius. 'Steffi, have you the document?'

Steffi slid papers from a file and handed them to the Professor.

'Are you ready to sign?' he asked.

'To sign what?'

'Your confession.'

'But I haven't done anything.'

'In the first place that is not true. You have brought this –' Gisevius brandished the book – 'this filth into the East German Republic.'

I looked at him open-mouthed.

'And in the second, it is irrelevant whether you have or have not done anything. Look around you.'

'You are between a cock and a hard place,' ventured Reiner from the floor.

'Will you for God's sake be quiet?' Steffi barked.

'You are pretending to be a private dick,' I said. 'And Steffi is…pretending to be a floozy. And Reiner is a gimp.'

'You are droll, Doktor,' said Reiner.

'Sign in the two places indicated,' Gisevius went on, smoothly.

'This is not real. You are playing at – at all this. This fantasy of crime and detection and *film noir*.'

'You have merely to sign.'

'Or what? What is your authority?' I asked. 'You could be anyone.'

'Worry about the fact that I am not, that I am I, Gisevius. Reiner, you will need after all the pliers.'

'This part I enjoy also,' said Reiner, lumbering to his feet.

'Hang on,' I said. 'Have you a pen?'

'Of course. It is one of your English pens – an Osmiroid.'

I signed in two places. Reiner returned to the filing cabinet, put away the toolbox and produced a bottle of Schnapps and some shot-glasses.

'A toast: to our fraternal co-operation,' said Reiner.

'To international Socialism,' said Gisevius.

'To us,' I said, looking at Steffi. She gave me a small smile, then came and sat on my knee.

*

I missed my plane home because I spent the night in the doorway of the apartment block in Kreutzberg waiting for Steffi to arrive. Best to travel separately, she said. There was much to explain. This she would do when we were reunited. At six a.m Irmgard approached on foot.

'Where's Steffi?' I asked.

Irmgard shrugged and opened the front door. She would have closed it on me but I pushed in after her.

'Irmgard, where is Steffi?'

'Isn't she with you?'

'Don't fuck about.'

'Very well. I don't know where she is. You can go now. Back to England, yes?'

The lift arrived. Again I pushed in after her.

'This is futile,' said Irmgard.

'I want to see for myself.'

Irmgard shook her head wearily. When we reached the flat she unlocked the door and gestured to me to go ahead. It was not quite light yet but I could see that the living room was empty. I went out on to the balcony. The pool had been drained. In it lay a recliner cushion and a pair of pink goggles. In the middle distance the Funkturm glittered in the dawn, pumping its cheery drivel into the homes of Actually Existing Socialists in the city next door.

When I went back into the living room Irmgard was

sitting on the settee with a young blonde girl in a grubby t-shirt. She lay with her head in Irmgard's lap. They were watching the early news with the sound off.

'Who's this?'

Irmgard did not look up. I repeated the question.

'This is my cousin Annaliese on a visit from the farm where she lives with her grandparents and tends to her pigs and geese. In other words, Richard, fuck off and mind your own business. No, I do not know where Steffi is. And if I did I would not tell you. And if you do not leave now I will call the police. Enjoy your flight.' The blonde girl giggled and stuck out her tongue.

I walked along the wall until I found a viewing platform. From there I stared across the death strip at the blocks of 1960s flats, each with its red-black-gold GDR flag on the balcony awaiting the May Day celebrations. Everything was in order.

When I got home, I waited. After a time I forgot I was waiting. I almost forgot Steffi for a while.

My career as an agent of the GDR failed to flower. I have never found out if anyone in the West even noticed my recruitment to the cause when the Stasi's papers were opened for scrutiny. No one has been in touch. Not our side, not their side. I flatter myself that I was one of the last to be caught in a honeytrap, though it is galling that no one seems to care. I would supply details of the political tendencies of fellow academics and poets, and of students, in exchange for not being exposed to the British authorities, and I would get to go on sleeping with Steffi with or without her 1940s costume.

What happened? We know what happened. The GDR collapsed. Gysi and the reforming wing of the SED were pushed aside in the rush to change and then to unity. And now there are Nazis all over the former East Germany and the Bundesrepublik is bankrupt. *Plus ça change*. People say they knew the Berlin wall was going to come down. They knew fuck all. They knew no more than me, and I knew *less* than fuck all – I, the agent, actual or imaginary, of a foreign power. Dignity demands that I be right in this regard at least. Who could bear to be the mere patsy of the degenerate phase of what-is-no-longer-historically-significant?

And now? Let's face it, who reads Mickey Spillane nowadays? Except a few freaks on eBay. As it happens, I've stocked up on original Spillanes. This April I'm taking my wares to a collectors' event being held somewhere in Mitte. You never know. It might be Gisevius. Just. It might be Reiner, bloated with bonhomie. Not Steffi, of course not, but if it is you, then, Liebchen, kiss me deadly.